MARLIN, DARLIN'

GARNET SULLIVAN LIVE FROM FLORIDA

BY

MARGARET JEAN LANGSTAFF

*A grisly murder at sea forms the
basis for this sizzling mystery
set in steamy east coast Florida,
featuring freelance reporter,
snoop and trouble-maker, Garnet Sullivan,
and a host of her bizarre, colorful friends . . .
a Gordian knot of a plot . . . .
sure to delight the most cerebral
mystery buffs as well as fans of
romantic comedy.*

ISBN 978-0-9702138-7-7

Cedar Hill Press LLC

August 2010

14260 W. Newberry Rd.
Newberry, FL 32669

The following is a work of fiction. Any resemblance to actual
people, places or events herein is unintended and coincidental.

ABOUT THE AUTHOR

Margaret Langstaff has written more than twenty books, both under her own name and as a ghostwriter for others, and countless feature articles and book reviews for prominent national periodicals, such as the *L.A. Times*, *Publishers Weekly*, *BookPage*, and the *L.A. Times Book Review* and *Business Page*. She is a former member of the National Book Critics Circle and former board member of the Book Industry Study Group.

Educated at the University of Florida (English, magna cum laud, Phi Beta Kappa), she grew up in Florida and knows the Florida scene, culture, flora and fauna—and *freaks*—like the back of her own hand.

While the characters and situations in her Florida novels are not based on actual people or events, they are, as it were, drawn from life and derive from her lifelong immersion in and keen observation of the strange, whacked-out and alluring land known as Florida.

TABLE OF CONTENTS

ONE

Hell bent south toward the inlet.

✠ ✠ ✠

Bubbles spewed from his mouth like the bright tail of an underwater comet. He roared through the light-dappled water in pursuit of a shadowy thing he would never overtake, skidding over the surface when the fish dove through waves, his Gore-Tex jacket snapping smartly in the warm morning breeze. The fish's great cone-shaped bill pierced the cool Gulf Stream, oblivious to the hook embedded in the back of its head. The fish swam forward as it always had. Blue, intent, elusive, forcing oxygenated water into heaving red gills. The line wound through the man's fingers, arms and legs, binding his body like crazy packing twine.

Or so I imagined, sitting at a traffic light after hearing the news on the radio that a fisherman in the marlin tournament off Jupiter Island had been pulled overboard by something he had hooked and was lost at sea. What was going through his mind as the fish keel-hauled the life out of him? What had he had for breakfast? What was the last thing he said to his wife?

The light changed and I put the car in first for the final lurch up the bluff to Building C. A pile of graded essays wrapped in rubber bands sat on the seat next to me.

At the end of the oyster shell drive, palm fronds drooped in the humid evening air. Three or four dull-eyed students stood underneath smoking. Most of my kids had day jobs and were beat when they came to class.

"Evening, Miz Sullivan." Mickey Bennett flicked an ash from his cigarette into a clump of palmettos.

The laggards streamed in behind me and took their seats with the rest of the linguistic virtuosos. When I set the bundle of essays on the desk, as a group the kids raised their heads from what they were doing.

I fumbled with my roll book. "Arbuckle?"

"Here."

"Bennett?" Of course he was here...

"Yeah."

"Davis?"

Jim Walker's skinny arm waved in the back. Walker was passing time as an auto mechanic until something better came along.

He grinned. "What'd you take for your Beetle?"

"Not for sale." I began returning their papers.

"Is that cute yellow convertible yours?" Amber Glenn asked accepting, reluctantly, a C minus for her exposition of the kitchen set-up system at the Pelican.

"What year is it?" LaTisha Mason groveled in her desk. LaTisha received a D plus for her explanation of the video rental system at the Minit Mart. So much for fines.

With a transition worthy of Stephen Colbert, I conducted the class's collective psyche back to the portal of learning. "Actually, the car's a '78. Which brings to mind Cassy Moran's

2

paper on the birth of her sister at home on the laundry room floor. I'd like Cassy to lead off our discussion tonight by reading her paper."

At break, over the whine of the spring peepers, I overheard a group of guys outside talking about the man the fish pulled overboard. Some of my kids were fishermen by trade. They brought in the red snapper, grouper, flounder and lobster for the fish markets and restaurants from West Palm Beach to Stuart. They were the drones, not the glamour boys, of the fishing industry.

"These rich shits go out to the blue water in a big ass boat they don't know how to handle."

"The Hatteras—a custom job—went dry off Daytona. Clean as a whistle. No sign of nothing."

"What was he doing out there alone, for chrissake?"

"Who the hell was it?"

"One a them shit-faced snowbirds."

I rose and stood in the doorway and motioned everyone back in. The fish story was grist for the other half of my livelihood. It might make a dinner for me and my dog. The papers up north loved this sort of color for four to six inch fillers. And the local mullet wrappers would take whatever scoops I delivered and run them under inch tall heads. Man Moby Dicks Self with Marlin?

Walker slid by with an embarrassed smile. "So you really don't want to sell your car? It'd make one class dune buggy, man."

I pointed to his seat.

✠ ✠ ✠

The wind off the ocean was balmy and sweet. I pulled the tie from my hair and let the breeze run through it. There were

3

few cars on the road. The sky was sprayed with light and ornamented with a crescent moon.

When I pulled into my parking space I saw Ringo's head in the window, asleep on the back of the couch. He jumped up when my headlights shot into the living room, barked and swung his long feathered tail back and forth. Together we crossed A1A and went down to the beach. The tide was out and foam from the waves fringed the water's edge. I tried to stay awake as Ring chose his targets.

A sheriff's car and a rescue van blew by, blue and red lights flashing, as we reached the crest of the dune on our way back, hell bent south toward the inlet. We skipped back over the two-lane blacktop, still warm from the sun.

The tape of my antique answering machine squeeled and jibbered rewinding and I took heart that I'd had several calls. Things had been slow the past few weeks. Instead of lifting my spirits, the good weather we'd had put me in a funk.

One less thing to be suicidal about. The tape continued to unreel the pitiable chronicle my life was becoming.

The editor of the *Stuart Times,* Fred Phillips, a dear man with a face like old newsprint, had called at 3:00 p.m. to "see what was new." Did I have anything on the pending sign ordinance? And was I covering the marlin tournament accident? "Call me ASAP, cutie. Ciou."

I had three more calls some time after that about the fishing accident from other Florida papers: the state desks of the *Gainesville Sun,* the *Tampa Tribune,* and the *Pensacola Post.*

I should have called them. It was breaking news. I was pathetic. No wonder editors felt they didn't have to pay me.

"Move over, Ring." I was worn to a nub. Missing an old boyfriend. I could put in four days on the fish story before I had to worry about teaching again. Assuming it would be worth the effort.

Just as I was drifting off, a squalling flock of sirens raced by, heading south on A1A, following the same trajectory the sheriff's car and rescue van had taken. I jumped out of bed with a hammering headache and began to throw on my clothes.

TWO

The alpine whisp of Certs.

✠ ✠ ✠

The lights were picked up by swirls of water where ocean and river converged, creating a crazy pinwheel effect in the night. I peered into the pale faces above the uniforms and came up empty. To one side, two people sat in an ambulance with the motor running and the headlights off. The badges were all facing the water. When I walked up, no one turned around or said hello, good-bye or get lost.

Then something like a manatee surfaced at the far ocean end of the jetty, heaved a large fin onto the embankment and hauled itself out of the water. A second thing of the same description followed.

"What are you looking for?" I said to a short sergeant.

"Who wants to know?"

A taller guy next to him turned toward the ambulance and pointed to the road with his thumb. The ambulance turned on its headlights, gunned the engine and rolled down the access road to A1A.

The two frogmen in flippers squished and squeeked toward us like aliens in a sci-fi movie. One of them was calling my name.

I'd know those legs anywhere.

"Well, well, well," he said, stopping a few inches from my face. The blue lights lit up a cool half-smile.

"Fancy seeing you here, Chester."

He yanked my ponytail and thumped off.

Having become adept at recovering from such interludes, I was able to grab the tanks of the second diver as he was about to pass me.

"Press." I waved my notebook like a gun.

Bernard Pruitt worked for the sheriff's department. He wasn't sure about the other guy. Bernard had been summoned to the scene to look for body parts, fishing tackle, weapons, whatnot. They didn't find anything, but it was dark and the water was rough. He kicked off his flippers, and strode over to a white and green van into which he dumped his tanks with a resounding clang.

"So what was with the ambulance?" I asked, falling into step with the sergeant. I guided him into a wide veering circle, away from the others.

He stopped. "Okay. You'll have to talk to the captain for details, but we sent a body to Riverfront Gen to be pronounced. Was missing an arm. Some lovebirds found it."

"Hold it, please. I represent several major newspapers." But he clammed up and walked off.

The diver in the van tipped a flipper to me as I drove by. Not a spectacular beginning, but I had been the sole member of the working press on the scene. I needed to call some news desks quick.

But I'd forgotten my phone.

It was just midnight. I could still make some morning papers. I felt around on the floor of the front seat and was

7

relieved to locate my laptop. I flew over the high-rise bridge to the mainland with the top down, the same bridge I'd crossed two hours before.

From the margins of my thoughts, the question of Chester's presence at the jetties buzzed at me like an annoying fly. Since he was a golf buddy of Lance Dawtry's, any number of explanations were possible. And he was a well-known SCUBA enthusiast, with mementos galore littering his public defender's office. They were short-handed and someone called him. It was that simple. But why hadn't he called me with the tip? Weren't we at least still friends?

As I wheeled into the parking lot at headquarters, a Channel 5 van with a transponder antenna sat out front. I grabbed my notebook and tape recorder and ran like a mad woman. The TV crew was setting up in the hallway and the talent was checking his hair in a mirror.

I stalled out at the phone booth down the breezeway. It was occupied by an older woman rummaging in her large purse. She looked up and smiled, revealing a dark gap where her teeth should have been. I double-timed it to the phone at the opposite end of the building. The muscles in my legs were stinging and taut when a door opened off the hallway and I slammed headlong into a man coming out of an office. The next thing I knew, I was sitting on the terrazzo.

"You hurt, Garnet?" Lance Dawtry asked, bending over.

Chinks of light glimmered around the edges of everything. He reeked of aftershave and Right Guard.

"Got the wind knocked outta you?" He put out a hand.

"Talk to me, Lance."

The alpine whisp of Certs guided me into his office. He and Chester had been together at some watering hole when this thing broke. The thought burned me up.

"What state was the body in?"

"Dead. Wet."

"Which arm was missing?"

"Left." He rolled his eyes to the ceiling and snapped fingers. "No! Right!"

"Okay, so it's just some soggy white guy, but off the record, who is it?"

He opened his mouth and his phone started ringing. His hand hovered in mid-air.

He closed his eyes and sighed. Pressed his palm against his forehead. A Mrs. Devaigne was wailing on him. Wouldn't let him get a word in. He shuffled through a hopeless mire of papers on his desk looking for something to write with, then motioned to me for my pen.

He repeated a number with a Miami area code, frowned and hung up.

"Who was that?"

"The lady whose husband evaporated from his 48 foot Hatteras in broad daylight today."

"Any connection to the body in question, Sheriff?" I mugged. Any minute they were going to come for him for the cameras.

"I don't know, Miz Sullivan." He pulled a tube of mints out of his jeans and peeled back the foil.

"But you aim to find out."

"Durn tootin', Missy." He got up to show me the door. An avalanche of cameras and people was hurtling down the hall.

I pulled the door to and asked if I could use his desk and phone to quickly file some stories. The crowd was at the door, milling around.

"I'll just be a minute." I looked square into his nice brown eyes.

He popped a mint into his mouth and smoothed his hair. "Just don't screw up my filing system."

Tampa and Jacksonville took it gratefully, and Miami, grudgingly. Jerry at the state desk there had to confer with

Ann at the city desk before I got the go ahead to transmit. Then they wanted to fool around with the lead. Wanted to put the fishing mishap upfront. Had some copy of their own they wanted to run. The whereabouts of Mr. Devaigne was hot stuff in Miami. Owned seventeen GM-Chevy-Cadillac dealerships in Florida, Georgia and the Carolinas. Lavish home on Biscayane Bay. And his wife was suing him for divorce in Dade County. Or trying to. She hadn't been able to have him served with papers yet. He kept disappearing.

✠ ✠ ✠

I stood in the parking lot trying to let my brain return to room temperature before striking out for home. It was almost 3:00 a.m. If I was lucky, I'd made three or four hundred dollars.

The parking lot was on a bluff overlooking the river causeway. Coconut palms ringed the area and their fronds clattered in the breeze. The lights on the bridge wore yellow aureoles of mist. Down below, the pungent aroma of low tide. When the breeze gusted, it was almost overwhelming.

I felt in my pocket for the yellow Post It on which I had jotted Mrs. Devaigne's phone number. I liked the way it felt. Crisp, snappy, useful.

Something in this tranquil scene moved and I started. A pale stream of smoke twirling upward from what I'd thought was a tree stump. A woman sat on a bench overlooking the bluff and leaned forward in a crouch. I thought of the odd older woman I'd seen in the phone booth, digging around in her enormous purse.

I got in my car wondering where Chester was, what he was doing. How he looked asleep.

THREE

A little black dress and a string of pearls.

✠ ✠ ✠

The preliminary autopsy report showed the dental records of David K. Devaigne matched the teeth of the corpse that was fished out of the inlet. Frogman Pruitt and the sarge hadn't mentioned the heavy gauge line the body was trussed with or I would have laid bets that would be the case. No one knew how the man lost his right arm, which had been wrenched from his shoulder like a wing from a roast chicken. And the rest of the unfortunate man's carcass looked as if it'd been pounded with a meat mallet. The coroner guessed the time of death was nine or ten yesterday morning. Cause of death: drowning. The complete report with blood and tissue analysis would come later, probably early next week.

After filing follow-ups with Tampa, Miami and Jacksonville, I passed the early afternoon pitching the story to some big papers in the North.

Mid-afternoon I received a call from Allison Highsmith that cleared up the Chester puzzle. He and Lance had attended one of her fundraisers at the Beach Club and had spent the evening swilling spirits for a worthy cause. Allison came from an old Port Oklawassa family with money and an inbred, stalwart sense of community responsibility. The Highsmith clan stamped out generations of civic leaders and champions of the underdog. Allison, who was my age, headed up several charitable causes in the area and sat on the national boards of a few.

Give her a little black dress, a string of pearls and a list of potential contributors and she could mint money. Today she had me on the line for a Save the Manatee dog walk.

"We have to have you and Ringo."

"I don't get it. You mean a whole bunch of people get together and walk their dogs? How do you make any money?"

"You pay to do it, sugar pie."

"I pay you to walk my dog?"

"Yes, because it's a party, dummy."

"Dogs aren't allowed on public beaches, Allison." Even though I snuck mine down there all the time.

"Don't worry about it. I've talked to Lance. He said they'd look the other way."

"That will be hard to do when two hundred dogs and their owners show up in one spot, won't it?"

She snorted. "Trust me on this, Garnet."

Then she said she was wondering, she just wanted to check and make sure so there'd be no misunderstanding, but would I mind if she asked Chester to go with her and Pookie, her Yorkie-Airdale mix, to this soiree.

"He doesn't have a dog."

"He can borrow Burgess, Dad's dog."

"Well, of course. Why not?"

"Are you sure? Absolutely?"

"Believe me, Allison. I really don't mind. Have fun."

She said last night he told her he was really committed to saving the manatee, that something had to be done. I wondered if at that point in the evening Chester knew a manatee from a goatee.

✠ ✠ ✠

On my way out the door for the grocery, I encountered a man coming up my walk. Vaguely intelligent eyes with a preoccupied glaze. Worn looking. Walked as if his back were stiff.

"Long trip up from Miami?" I hazarded.

He squinted in the angling light of the setting sun. "About four hours. Yeah. That turnpike is dull as hell."

Randy Trigg had been sent by Miami to see what the real story was with the demise of Dave Devaigne, car dealer extraordinaire. I directed him inside to cool his heals with Ringo until I returned from the store. When I came back half an hour later, Ringo had him in an orangutan embrace on the couch.

"I'm sorry," I said, finally. "Would you like a coke or something? "A beer maybe?" We both popped a can and he kicked back.

"Some interesting developments today," he said, studying his battered running shoes.

As he recounted them, it became clear it was all news to me. For in Miami, in a fracas of allegations, suits and motions, the Devaigne family had summarily fractured on the news that daddy was dead. Julie Devaigne, the estranged wife, wanted to bring the body back for services and burial.

13

But the two Devaigne kids, in their twenties and from a previous marriage, immediately filed a motion asking for an injunction to block her from obtaining the remains. Just before Randy left Miami this afternoon, Julie Devaigne's lawyers had filed a countersuit.

"On what grounds?"

"Fraud. And wrongful death."

Trigg was sprawled across my sofa in a jaded world-weariness that I found a shade self-conscious and cultivated.

"Of course. These would be civil suits."

"Get your mind outta the gutter, Miz Sullivan."

A telltale vein in my forehead began to throb.

Apologetically he added, "Actually, you may not be so off of the mark, if you're thinking manslaughter, homicide, that sort of thing. It happens."

"About you or Devaigne?"

He saluted me with his empty beer can and set it on the end table. "Thanks."

✠ ✠ ✠

That evening, over a plate of homemade spaghetti, I watched TV. The phone was silent and I was glad for the time to myself. I had a glass of wine, brushed Ringo, did my nails. Vegged. About nine, as I was having one of my periodic guilt spasms over what I was going to teach next week, I switched to the Discovery Channel.

Where they got the footage, I don't know, but I tuned in to a program already in progress at the point in which a diver is attacked by a shark. A native islander in the Carribbean, in white briefs and scuba gear, is putzing around a coral reef with a spear gun. Out of nowhere a lethal looking blade of a creature appears and grazes the guy's shoulder with his jaws. The shark is longer and wider than the man by yards. The man spins around in a column of fizzing air. His mouthpiece is bobbling loose and he is doubled over in pain, grasping his mask. The thing does a quick hairpin turn and comes back, scissoring at the man's torso with layered rings of teeth. Blood jets and darkens the water.

I punched the volume up. But the documentary shifted and was now off on another tangent having to do with sharks. It had been a *National Geographic* equivalent of a snuff movie. The whole thing made me sort of ashamed of myself.

I threw the dishes in the dishwasher and snapped Ring to his leash. I let him loose at the beach across the street and we walked a couple of miles under a star swept sky. I had copy to write for several papers and their Sunday editions. I also had follow-up calls to make on the David Devaigne news nova that was lighting up my life. If I played my cards right, the whole thing could put me in the black again.

Randy Trigg could prove to be a pain in the neck. The *Herald* had a syndicated news service. If he scored before I did, it would eliminate the need for my stories with several papers I had standing by. I wished I hadn't called Miami at all. But any delay would have only put them off for a day or two.

The way that shark had come out of nowhere and savaged that diver ambushed my thoughts repeatedly. I waded into the surf and felt my toes curl up.

Ringo chased a gaggle of insomniac sand pipers and thrilled to their squeels. I whistled a few times and he braked and turned around. Chester should get a dog. It would be good company for him and impose some sort of routine on his evenings.

The eleven o'clock news confirmed what Randy Trigg had told me earlier: the David K. Devaigne Family had ruptured into two factions and were suing each other right and left.

The shots they flashed of his wife and kids were a surprise. His wife must have been in her early thirties when the photo was taken. Her hair and outfit seemed recent. The two kids, a young man and woman, had been photographed at the Bal Harbor boat show last year on the foredeck of a Hatteras similar to the one their dad had piloted out of the inlet. They were in their late twenties. His wife was blond, they were brunette.

Devaigne's general managers in Naples and Augusta were interviewed briefly and said that the marlin tournament planned a memorial service for Devaigne at sea on Sunday.

Something was up to warrant all this ink and airtime. At least the news director for Channel 5 had gone out on a limb. It would be hard for them to just drop it now.

✠ ✠ ✠

I was sitting up in bed in the dark with my heart thundering and the phone at my ear.

"Who is this?" It was a man's voice. Caustic. Confrontational.

"I beg your pardon?"

"Who is this? You heard me."

"Well, just who the hell is this?" I snarled.

The voice guffawed and then collapsed in a coughing fit. But I'd had enough of a sample.

"What're ya'll doin?"

"Sleeping." If I had any self respect, I'd just hang up.

"Chester?"

"What?"

"Where are you?"

"None of your business."

"Chester, go to sleep. Please."

"I will always love you," he said evenly. Then he hung up.

I lay awake for an hour afterward, imagining him reeling around his condo, changing CD's, pumping up the volume. Filling his glass.

FOUR

A turnpike-borne pestilence.

✠ ✠ ✠

The scent of jasmine from the night before lingered in the breeze. I rounded the banyan-shaded curves on Riverside Drive, weaving in and out of the dappled light. As I passed the homes strung next to one another like pastel beads, people were picking up their newspapers in their driveways, getting into their cars for church or the beach or boat, checking the sky for weather portents. They wore the bland weekend faces of the well rested and financially secure.

The back road to the airport took me by the public marina, a small operation tucked into a brackish canal not far from the intercoastal. Light sailboats and a bright assortment of ski and fishing craft were resting among the pilings. A brown pelican held court with floating seagulls at his feet atop a post near the gas pumps.

The screen door to the harbor master's office slammed as I drove by and I caught a glimpse of Randy Trigg marching toward the docks. What this turnpike-borne pestilence was doing there was not immediately clear to me.

I downshifted and pulled into a parking space a few yards distant and watched him walk down the boardwalk. He had seen me.

"Hey. What's up?" He leaned a forearm on my car door.

"Just out for a drive," I said. "Taking the air."

Good day for it," he said, looking me in the eye.

Chasms of information separated us. I searched his face for signs of superiority and smugness, or even sympathy.

"How's the story coming?"

"I was just going to ask you the same thing," he said, grinning. One of his front teeth had been capped shabbily.

"Nothing new here."

"Here either." He rubbed his eyes as if he had a headache.

"What are you snooping around here for?"

"The sheriff said they were towing Devaigne's boat back this morning. This is where they told them to tie it up."

"No sign of it yet?"

"It's still early."

I started my car. "I'll be back."

✣ ✣ ✣

Trigg and I had to form some sort of alliance, as distasteful as it would be to both of us. Separately we were only going to be getting in the other's hair. Maybe he was smarter than he looked, but I thought he would benefit at least as much as I would by joining forces. Trouble was, I wasn't sure how I was going to get paid fairly in such an arrangement. If I became, as far as Miami was concerned, just an adjunct to Trigg, my revenue streams from the other newspapers would dry up and I'd be left with Miami paying me for hours worked.

But consider the alternative. Give up, move on to something else? Like what?

On my way back to the marina from the airport newsstand with a raft of Sunday papers, I read as I drove. Tampa had given my piece on Devaigne ten column inches on the front page of the state section. Jacksonville had done the same and had run a shot alongside it that one of their staff photographers had taken of Devaigne's yacht in Daytona. The photo considerably juiced up their coverage. The boat's name was *O, Julie!*, for the wife who was chasing Devaigne all over to have him served with divorce papers. Acres of sleek white fiberglass with elegant navy trim. From the angle at which it was shot, it seemed to be a hundred feet long.

I wondered how this big mother was going to squeeze into the tiny municipal marina.

I tossed the two papers in the backseat, satisfied that the Garnet Sullivan byline was slugged in and not butchered into something like Granite Soloman.

About the same nanosecond, I ran off the road into a muck-filled drainage ditch. The wheels bounced and the engine stalled out as the bumper banged into a culvert. Just for good measure, because I had not been wearing my seatbelt, I banged my forehead on the windshield. A thesaurus of profanity blew though my mind. I started the motor again and tried to back up. The car rolled about eight inches before the drive wheel started spinning in place.

I took a deep breath. With my hazard lights on, I opened the Miami paper.

It didn't take long to realize Miami had made me a mere sidebar to Randy Trigg's involved piece. They gave him half of the front page of the city section and it bumped and spread out across half of another page. My bit had been buried inside and compressed to the point of nonsense.

Trigg had filed this opus before he left Miami. Serious research had gone into it, a number of people were quoted, public records cited. He was the current world expert on the public and private affairs of David K. Devaigne.

"Miz Sullivan? Need some help?"

I looked up into the earnest face of Jim Walker from EH101. "Want some extra credit, Jim?"

"Will you look at this," he said admiringly. He squatted by the back wheels and whistled.

Walker had on his blue mechanic's uniform with "Jimmy" embroidered in red on the pocket. Looking over his shoulder I could see he had a female passenger.

Before I knew it, we were riding three abreast in the front seat of his old Pontiac, hastening down US 1.

"Are those glasspaks, Jim?"

"Yeah," he yelled, smiling at the road.

After a bit of pathetic mewling on my part, Walker had volunteered to get a tow truck from the dealership and have my car delivered to the marina.

Between us sat his girlfriend, Bunny Knapp. Bunny was a cashier in the service department.

"I been thinking about going back to school, taking some courses!" she said at the top of her lungs. "Got to find somebody to watch my kids at night first!" Bunny was a cute pint-sized spikey bottle-blonde.

We came to a tingling stop in front of the marina.

"I saw your article in the mullet wrapper this morning, Miz Sullivan," Walker said. "That's really something. Too bad and all. I knew that man."

"You did?"

"Yeah." He smiled broadly and shook his head. "That was the guy who was trying to buy out Fendermann."

"What?"

"The Devaigne guy who fell outta his boat and drowned, or whatever happened to him. He's been coming around our store asking Travis Fendermann what he'd take for it."

Bunny fidgeted. "If you dudes would write more business, Mr. Fendermann might not have to listen to people like him."

"Like whom?"

"The rich guy that fell outta his boat. That Mr. Devaigne from Miami," she said pointing toward the water.

I followed her finger to the *O, Julie!* A duck-shaped tug nudged her from behind. She was a little smaller than the photo in the paper had suggested, but not by much.

"Business is slow," Jim said with a hang-dog face. "But I ain't writing estimates for phony repairs, neither."

"Something about that guy was skuzzy," Bunny said, more to Walker than to me. "I'm not glad he died, but I am glad Mr. Ferndermann won't have to be bothered with him anymore."

The harbor master's screen door banged shut and Trigg and a man in a Greek fisherman's cap loped by. Randy had a couple of notebooks sticking out of the waistband of his shorts and a camera slung over his shoulder.

✠ ✠ ✠

When I reached the *O, Julie!* at dockside, Trigg and two Coast Guard types were having a disagreement that bode to veer out of control. One of the officers stood off to the side on the aft deck holding a crook-shaped docking pole like a jousting lance. The other one listened, arms folded across his chest, to a fiercely well-informed Randy Trigg expound on public access, freedom of the press and the First Amendment. Behind him the harbor master nodded in furious agreement.

"Fascists," he muttered as I walked up.

Trigg paused.

"Don't let me interrupt."

He scowled and returned to his brief.

"So the bottom line, gentlemen, is you don't let me board and have a look around, fine. I'll have your butts in court tomorrow morning on the FOIA."

The top gun Coast Guardman's eyes were black dots in a blanched face. He put his hands together and cracked his knuckles. Their report resounded like automatic gunfire in the quiet little harbor. He had big hands, big shoulders and big hairy arms. Surely he wouldn't hit a member of the press.

"Randy," I said, tugging at his revolting fishnet tank top. "Time out."

"Be right back, gentlemen."

The two Coast Guard guys traded looks and resumed tying up.

"What the hell are you doing, Randy?"

He opened his mouth but nothing came out.

"And by the way, it was pretty sleezy of you to play so dumb about the Devaigne family."

He cut his eyes to the left. "Oh that." Then taking me by the arm, "Work with me on this. This is going to be big. I need help."

"And I need help, too, friend."

"I'll share a byline with you on everything filed from here."

"Finally, my name in print."

"And you'll get a per diem, all expenses covered. That sort of thing."

I closed my eyes.

He squeezed my shoulders. "Okay! And a guaranteed fee for a month."

"How much?"

"I'll have to ask my editor."

23

"Make it worth my while."

Returning with Trigg to the yacht where he aimed to deliver yet another salvo of press law in the direction of the Coast Guard, I noticed a sheriff's car had pulled up.

"Listen. Lay off these sailors," I advised. "They have to turn the boat over to the sheriff's department. Once that happens, things may lighten up."

FIVE

A burned-out case.

✠ ✠ ✠

There's something about a dog when you're down in the dumps. I stared at the monitor as Ringo slept on my foot. The phrase *Am I blue?* trailed through my mind like a ribbon. It was from a song, in a black woman's voice, but I was at a loss to name the artist. The ocean roared across the street.

I glanced at the unopened pack of cigarettes on the side of my desk. I'd walked to the Minit Saver, not so far really, but walked in the dark all the same, to buy them. Ringo was with me. So what?

Things were not going well.

Jim Walker never came back with my car. When I called, no one at the dealership knew anything about it. And girlfriend Bunny Knapp wasn't listed.

Randy Trigg had taken me home after a two-hour vigil, during which he turned into an irritating know-it-all. "Most of those low lives are on meth. You can't count on them," he pontificated. "You surprise me, Sullivan. Such naivete' for a veteran reporter. Must be the small town, huh? I guess you don't see much here, eh?"

It didn't help my mood that while we were waiting for the ephemeral, now crack-head, Walker, that Chester happened by with the strange old bird I'd seen at sheriff's headquarters.

Chester honked and, minus the hack, I walked over. His face was red and he was higher than a kite.

"Hey, babe," he said.

"Hi," I said, my arms hanging helplessly at my sides.

"What's going on?"

"Same-old same-old."

"Meet Missus Bettina Bassett," he said, nodding to the burned-out case sitting next to him in the passenger's seat.

Miss Bettina nodded and smiled vacantly. The lights were on, but nobody was home at Bettina's.

"I am representing Miz Bassett," Chester said, arching an eyebrow. "Rather, our honorable Public Defender's office is representing her. That would be more correct to say." He stifled a burp.

"How nice."

"Know a guy named Jim Walker? A mechanic?"

"Why?"

"Just wondered." Then he screeched off.

As he careened around the curve under the railroad overpass, his car backfired and expelled a cloud of smoke. I fully expected him to be arrested before the day was over.

✠ ✠ ✠

Twirling a cigarette, my eye alighted on a dab of yellow. Julie Devaigne's home phone number, but what to do with it?

Please leave a message. A kid's voice on the recorder.

"Garnet Sullivan calling again for Mr. Fendermann. It is

quite urgent. One of your employees has disappeared with my car. Please call me as soon as you possibly can." I lit the cigarette without inhaling.

What did Chester want with Walker? He could have been picked up for something, of course, and be a client. Or he could have already been in trouble before he offered to help me get my car out of the ditch.

I called the city and county jails. Nobody had heard of him. I stubbed out the cigarette butt in a coffee saucer.

A memo from the *Herald* directed to Randy Trigg ground out of the fax machine next to me, followed by a photograph. I guessed this tacitly meant they were going to hire me.

Streaks and all, it was still clearly Julie Devaigne and a young good-looking guy. Leaving a club. Loved her little dress. With legs like that she could get away with thigh-high hemlines. She was in profile, ducking. He faced the camera, bug-eyed.

"The photo was taken last night at Club Folio on South Beach," the memo said. "Mrs. Devaigne and Monty Mossbach. Owns Mossbach Nurseries. Big sod supplier. Thousand acres near Homestead."

Not exactly the grieving widow. The dress was black, but come on. She and the kids were still fighting over the body. It was chilling in the morgue at Riverfront General waiting for the dust to settle.

I dialed Randy's efficiency at the Palms.

"Speaking," he said, half asleep.

"You better come over."

It wouldn't surprise me if he hopped in the car and took off for Miami tonight.

I picked up the paperback I'd found at the Minit Market earlier. On the cover, a color photograph of a Great White. The book fell open to a picture of the harmless little hammerheads found in shallow water around here. Surf fisherman reeled them in every day and left them to die on the sand.

In the middle of the book was a two-page color spread of a beached shark the size of a whale. Several shirtless men stood around it gaping. Its mouth was open, baring rows of teeth the size of a man's hand. A thick rope led away from its mouth and trailed off outside the frame of the photograph.

✠ ✠ ✠

The night was tarry black, not a star anywhere. A warm front hovered over our part of the map. The water smacked the bow of the Boston whaler like a soft hand on a drum. Crossing the river, I'd had to vector in from buoy to buoy. Of course I'd had plenty of advice from Skipper Trigg. The prevailing winds, effective drift. A long discourse on how to repair a sheared pin.

"Enough, Randy."

"This was your idea, Sullivan. Not mine."

I cut the motor and we coasted past the gas pumps. One flood light burned over the door to the office. It tapered off into a semi-circle pool of light in the empty parking lot. The office itself was dark.

"Now what?"

"Grab ahold of the pilings and pull."

"Shit. All the way?"

We made smooth headway halfway through, pulling hand over hand along the docks. Then laughter sounded from a tied up sailboat. Easy listening music from a radio wafted toward us. Someone sneezed.

"There are people in there," Trigg whispered astutely.

"I know."

"Let's get outta here."

"You surprise me, Randy. All your worldly bullshit and still such coward."

We slipped past the sailboat and several similar craft, no sweat. Then Trigg sputtered and gave out.

"What's the matter, Randy?"

"Wait a minute." He was breathing heavily. "I'm doing all the work here, Sullivan," he gasped, heaving for breath.

Then the drone of a distant motor impinged on our subtle intentions. The water became ruffled and a breeze lifted our hair. An airboat was coming along the channel. The huge fan-like contraption mounted on its stern beat the air like a furious airplane prop. When it came around the bend closest to us, overhung with mangrove, it was a gale force air displacement machine. Suddenly it blasted a dense flock of dozing seagulls out of the bushes into the damp night air. They screamed in fright and disappeared into the dark.

An unnerving void engulfed me. Black empty space had replaced Randy. My partner in crime had vanished with the gulls. "Trigg!" I sputtered into the dark.

"What?" said a voice next to my knee. A splash of water hit me in the face.

"Don't ever do that again!"

"What's on the bottom here?" he asked with a rising whine. "It's gooey and squishy!"

"Just stay in and pull." It was like Bogart pulling Bacall in the *African Queen*, except there were no leeches and the male lead was a half-wit in a fishnet tank top. If the tide had been out, it would have been tough to do.

"Trigg? Can you swim?" He could fall in a hole on the bottom.

"Why?"

"Look out for that manatee."

Randy hissed like a snake. "You're gonna get me killed, Sullivan!"

The yacht looked as if it were tied up in yellow ribbon. It towered above us by at least ten feet of sheer white fiberglass.

"What do you suggest now, Sullivan?"

"Wade around it. Look for a diving platform or a ladder. And watch for the drop-off into the slip."

✠ ✠ ✠

"Sullivan?" He was standing over me on the yacht.

"You can call me Garnet, Randy."

"On the other side. I'll meet you there."

I slid our little anchor into the water and eased over the side of the whaler. The water was warm and sulfurous. Another boat was tied up close on the leeward side of the yacht. Why ask for trouble? After wading around the stern of the yacht, I found it. The last rung of an aluminum ladder was a foot and a half above the water line.

I ducked under the webbing of crime scene tape as Randy gave me a hand. "Oh, Julie."

Everything was first class and brand new. The teak hadn't even been polished. Strips of pristine chrome twinkled in the dark. The blue indoor/outdoor carpet smelled as if it'd just come from the factory.

"We could get arrested for this."

"Don't think about it."

I tried the door to the cabin. It was open.

"I'll keep an eye out."

"Stay right here, Randy."

Inside I found a light switch. Behind the first bulkhead was a galley with a stove, fridge and booth that would seat four. As I began to open the fridge, I caught myself. This had all been so spur-of-the-moment.

I used my wet shirt-tail to open the fridge. It was full of beer and frozen bait. A big ziplock with enough grass to make a salad for two.

30

Behind the galley was a room with bunks on either side. Behind that, the master suite. King sized bed. Track lighting. Sound system. Built-in desk and drawers. I took my shirt off so I could use both hands without worrying about prints. On the desk, charts, fishing guides. Magazines, *Car & Driver, Auto News, Fortune*. Credit card receipts. In a shallow drawer to the right, a baggy. White Powder. Pipette.

The deep drawer underneath was full of magazines. The Lotos-Eaters, a new one to me. Flipped open to people with outsized private parts performing gymnastic feats in pairs and three-somes. The drawer was jammed with different issues of the same magazine. Buried in the middle of the stack was a cache of candid snapshots taken aboard this very yacht. Assorted positions of repose and impalement. Under the magazines were some odd anatomical-shaped battery operated appliances. Spare batteries.

"You won't believe it."

"Tell me."

"Help me with this." I lifted the lid to one of two large bait boxes in the aft section. Dead whiting floating around, belly up.

A cat meowed in the dark.

"Randy. Check this out." I held the lid up on the other bait box. Slabs of red meat packed in dry ice. Crudely filleted tuna and bonito.

"What's that for, a cookout?"

He followed me to the stern. An enormous electric winch. Metal cable. Huge block and tackle.

"What the hell was he fishing for?"

"How old was that guy, Randy? Didn't you say sixty-seven?"

"What's that crap all over your shirt? Your hands too. You're shining, Sullivan."

SIX

Allison`s whaler.

✠ ✠ ✠

Bottles and tubes lined my kitchen countertops and glistened in the glow from my front porch light. Lighter fluid, baby oil, Vaseline, kerosene. Solvents and lubricants. Anything I could think of. The tough part was that I had to work in the dark. The stuff didn't show up in normal light. My hands and arms were growing red and irritated from all the rubbing.

We had left the whaler at Allison Highsmith's dock and walked back across the island to my place. She never knew it was missing. Trigg had some sinister theories about my iridescence. Ever since we'd walked in the door, he'd been on the phone to Miami. Ringo, confused by our late hour activity, came and went, sniffed at me and whined. From the kitchen, it seemed Randy was doing more listening than talking. Finally, he hung up.

"What'd they say? What's going on?"

"I think it's coming off a little."

"Easy for you to say."

"It's lighter."

"Lighter, meaning less of it? Or lighter, meaning I'm brighter?" I dribbled more baby oil down my forearms as the phone began to ring. "Get that, will you?"

"A Bunny Knapp, for you," he said, dropping the receiver on the sofa and shuffling into the downstairs powder room.

The connection was bad. She sounded as if she were continents away. But it boiled down to this: don't worry, your car's all right. It would be returned. "When?"

An electrical storm of noise answered me.

"Bunny, where are you? Where's Jim?"

A child began to cry in the background and then the line went dead. I was left with a dial tone and the hollow sound of my own breath in the receiver.

When I hung up, Randy was standing before me looking gray and peaked. "I'm going to pack it in. Sun's coming up." He began gathering together his notebooks and jacket. "They want me back in Miami for a few days."

I glared at him but it had no observable effect.

"I'll be in touch," he said on his way out the door.

A rosy glow illuminated the sea oats at the top of the dunes across the street. The birds were tuning up. Traffic was picking up on A1A. What the two of us had done the previous night, the things we'd seen, seemed impossible in the context of daylight. Gum in the gears of polite society.

"Randy! Wait!" I ran out to his car.

He leaned out the window, his last shred of patience slipping away.

"Do you think it's a good idea to drive all that way without sleep?"

"What?"

"When will you be back?"

"By Wednesday, I hope." He wasn't looking at me. His mind was elsewhere.

33

"What was the matter with that guy?"

Now he looked at me. Then he looked away. "I don't know. Sick. Weird. Who knows?" he said, turning back to me with a sheepish grin.

"Hurry, okay?"

✠ ✠ ✠

After a promising dawn, the sky had turned to the color and consistency of dirty laundry. I was too beat to be much good at anything, so I tried to sleep in and cogitate between naps. I had calls into Lance and Chester. Fendermann's office called and left a message on the machine, which I decided not to acknowledge. I didn't know what kind of trouble Walker was in and didn't want to add to his problems. I tried to make do with Bunny's assurances.

Allison Highsmith called about four and wanted to meet for a drink at the Ocean Grill. The sound of her voice was cheering and I felt myself relax as we traded wisecracks and gossip. I told her a friend had borrowed my car and she offered to pick me up.

The crowd at the Grill was light and well-behaved. I'd showered and put on make-up, a pair of jeans and a knit top. I felt civilized again. We nursed our pinot grigio and stared out the bay window at the surf. Long shadows stretched from the dunes toward the water.

"See the porpoises?"Allison said.

A school was hunting bait fish in shallow water. A burst of spray followed by a tidy fin, one after the other. Sometimes two or more were synchronized in their swim and broke water together. I don't know why this made me think of Chester.

"Garnet. Hey. Are you okay?"

"Of course. Are you?"

She threw back her head and laughed. Everyone at the bar, as if on cue, turned and looked. She motioned to the bartender with her wine glass for another round. Allison was a happening kind of gal. She lent a room the impression something important was going on, however dull and ordinary everyone else seemed to be.

Turned out that top of Allison's mind was publicity for the Save the Manatee Dog Walk. She was convinced I should head up the effort. I was unconvinced.

"You love dogs, work for newspapers and can write a good lead." She took a sip of wine. "You have to, Garnet. I haven't asked you to do anything in a year."

I studied her over the rim of my glass. Lustrous brunette hair, dark eyes. "Are you still going with Chester?"

"That's the plan."

"He's agreed to go?" It was nearly two months away. Chester was allergic to long term commitments.

"Yes."

"Okay, I will do the print publicity. Find one of your disk jockey admirers to handle radio and TV."

"That's fair, I guess."

I reached for a cigarette. "So what else is new?"

"Daddy had his car stolen yesterday. Have you heard about that? Right out of the driveway at home in broad daylight."

"That beautiful burgundy Mercedes?"

"Merlot, really. Yes. Flipped him out."

"Lance know anything?"

She leaned forward. "Don't say where you got this, but a deputy let it drop that enough late model cars have been boosted recently to make them think it's organized."

"Is that right?"

"When did you start smoking again?"

✠ ✠ ✠

Evening was settling in when Allison dropped me by my place. "Your hands and arms are simply radiant. Are you using a new lotion?"

"Just something I picked up at CVS on sale."

After she left, as I was fumbling at the door with my keys, an eerie feeling came over me. I slowly became convinced someone was nearby, watching me. I glanced at the date palms to my left. They were motionless. "Ring? You inside there?" I jabbed my key at the lock and it jammed in upside down. He must be upstairs sleeping. I yanked at the key and it came loose suddenly, throwing me off balance away from the porch light. My shining hands and arms shook as I sorted through the keychain. The pink oleander blossoms to the right of the door trembled. A long branch moved from side to side.

"Who is it?" I folded my arms over my chest. "Who's there?" I started backing down the walk to the parking lot. With a whooshing noise, the oleander branches suddenly split apart and a man bolted out of them toward me, head low, the whites of his eyes bulging, his arms whirling in a crazed effort to get hold of me. My heart stopped with a thud and a shriek ripped out of my gut like a wild animal. I spun around and tore across the blacktop with a scream spiraling out of my lungs loud enough to wake the dead. I did not stop sprinting or screaming until I reached the other end of the parking lot and the front door of a neighbor whose lights were on. By then Ringo was giving hue and cry and lights had flashed on up and down the rows of townhouses.

I banged with both of my fists. At last the door opened and I fell against the tanned chest of Vito Bellini, a retired biology professor and widower, clad in his boxer shorts. "What is this? Are you all right?" He pulled me inside and slammed the door. My breathing was jagged and my chest was about to explode.

"Nine one-one! Call it!"

✠ ✠ ✠

When the sheriff's department arrived, Mr. Bellini and I had consumed half a bottle of Chianti. I was wrapped in Mrs. Bellini's chartreuse chenille bathrobe with fist-sized red roses on the front. His silver poodle Mimi was in my lap.

The uniformed guys showed up with Ringo. They'd gone over my condo with a microscope and could come up with nothing more than footprints around the oleander. A few scattered pink flowers.

"At least I'm not imagining it."

The deputy in charge looked at me quizzically. "Did you think you were?"

"Of course not. It was just so frightening. Such a terrible surprise."

"Is there any reason you can think of that someone might want to scare you?"

"No." The light was dim in the Bellini living room. I kept my arms up the sleeves of the robe.

"We'd like you to come down to HQ and give us a composite."

"It was probably just a prowler." Still, I didn't want to spend the night alone in the condo.

Ringo and I rode in the backseat of the cruiser over the causeway bridge, up US 1, across Hibiscus and into the reserved section of the sheriff's parking lot. Ring sat up in the back seat next to me like a person and gazed indolently out the window at the passing sights. In the heat of the evening and the enclosed space, it was a trial to continue wearing the late Mrs. Bellini's bathrobe.

Lance was behind the desk looking over the dispatcher's shoulder when we walked in. He found the little pageant Ringo and I made quite colorful, most amusing. While he was trying to think of something smart to say, my professional instincts kicked in.

"What's going on with all these car thefts, Sheriff?"

He picked up a piece of paper from the dispatcher's desk and studied it. His cowlick was up at the back of his part and a five o'clock shadow gave him a grizzled Clint Eastwood aspect.

"What brings you here, Miz Sullivan? Or were you just roaming around the neighborhood in your bathrobe and decided to stop in?"

"Anything happening with the Devaigne situation, Lance? You must have the blood and tissue analysis by now. What's the coroner say?"

A deputy came over with a handful of papers and nodded down the hall. "Follow me, please."

Lance kept his eye on his reading material. "Stop by before you leave," he said quietly without looking up.

✠ ✠ ✠

I poured over the page, fascinated. A round tanned face, no eyebrows. Short thinning brown hair. Large facial creases falling away from the average nose. Round dark eyes encased in sclera as thick as cooked egg whites. Tee-shirt, brown pants. Heavy set. Medium height. Early middle-age. Caucasian with possible Mediterranean lineage somewhere.

I sat next to the artist and watched my nightmare rendered into a simple pencil sketch. I had never seen such a man before, and yet had seen him everywhere. He resembled every tradesman—plumber, electrician, gardener—I'd ever seen on the island.

The deputy next to me shrugged and stood up. "This is going to be tough."

"I guess so."

"We'll call you in a few days. Maybe we'll have some lineups for you to look at, some photos, I don't know."

"Right."

"Meantime, anybody you can stay with?"

"Not really, but I'll be all right."

"Well, keep your doors locked. The outdoor lights on. Call us if anything suspicious comes up. That dog any good?" Ring had collapsed on the floor like a folding table and was snoring.

Lance drove us home around 9:00. The sky had cleared and the stars had come out. I watched his gallant profile in the lights from passing cars. It was a face the cameras loved. He was everybody's idea of the good guy in the white hat.

He admitted to the car thefts. They were on the case, he said. Had some leads. Were working with St. Lucie County. Suspected a chop shop had been set up inland out in the weeds. That the cars were being sold for parts.

"Don't print it yet, though, Garnet."

"Why?"

"Just don't. We're not home free."

"Why chop up beautiful new cars? What a waste."

"Lot a money in parts."

He stalled me on the coroner's report. But he said Devaigne's death was probably going to be ruled accidental.

"What's the hold up, then?"

"There's not a hold up. The doc hasn't finished the paperwork is all."

"So the body's still in the morgue?"

39

"For the time being."

"Drugs?"

"Don't quote me."

He walked me to my door and poked around in the shrubbery. Put his hands on his hips and shook his head.

"What?"

"What are you up to now, Garnet?"

"What's that supposed to mean?"

"And what's under that bathrobe?"

"Oh, Lance, you old pervert."

SEVEN

The artist's rendering of the assailant.

✠ ✠ ✠

Barricaded behind my bedroom door, I sat cross legged on the bed and sifted scraps of paper and notes into piles. I had the phone beside me, hoping Chester would call before it got too late. Into a pile on my right, I put all of my unpaid bills. On my left, I stacked the stories I'd filed that I hadn't invoiced yet.

At the foot of the bed on the right corner were my notebooks filled with stuff I still had to write up and try to file somewhere. And a little off from it, notes that I was holding strictly for the *Herald*, according to my agreement with Trigg. Next to the notes, at the center of the foot of the bed, were my lesson plans and textbook. Across from that, on the left corner of the foot of the bed, was a well-thumbed copy of *The Golden Guide to Sharks,* some clips on shark fishing, Randy's piece in the Sunday paper, and glossy propaganda pieces that sheriff's department put out in the schools on the dangers of drugs.

No wonder I was confused.

In my hand I held a photocopy of the artist's rendering of my attacker. Provisionally, I tossed it into the notes for the *Herald*.

"No, Ring. Sit." He'd insinuated his head like a spatchula under the bills. "Stay, Ring." He wagged his tail and Macy's and the plumber sailed to the floor.

Nothing about the Devaigne thing was pretty but his widow. This crud on my arms, which was at last fading somewhat, had turned my tee-shirt black in splotches when it dried. I should throw my tee-shirt on a pile too, but which one?

The auto thefts were connected to Fendermann, who was in some sort of financial bind. And he had some truck with David Devaigne in the days or weeks before the marlin tournament. Jim Walker was like the canary in the coal mine. His silence was ominous. Did someone know he was talking to me?

Devaigne had legions of people dependent on him and was prowling around for more, if he'd been interested in Fendermann's dealership. His drug and sexual peccadilloes could have been no secret to his wife. According to Randy's piece in the *Herald*, she was suing him for half of everything they had acquired since they'd been married, trying to slip through a loophole in a pre-nuptial agreement.

I swallowed hard and dialed Chester's number. The phone rang seven times.

"Speaking."

"It's me."

"Who is this?" he drawled like Chester on *Gunsmoke*.

"Jennifer Lopez."

"WHO?"

"Hillary Rodham Clinton."

"Come on."

"Mother Theresa? Who do you want it to be?"

"Don't you have anything better to do than bother a tired public servant?"

✠ ✠ ✠

Ringo ran ahead of us into the dark and circled back when he'd reached the limit of the invisible radius that tied him to me and made him my dog. The sand was cool and phosphorescent under our bare feet and we kicked at it to make sparks fly. When I turned to talk to him over the roar of the incoming tide, I had an urgent desire to kiss him behind his ear. But I didn't.

"You're too smart for your own good. Way too smart for a girl."

"Oink." I'd told him what I was working on. And about the man at my door. We listened to the heavy surf make mincemeat of the shore.

"Do you ever wonder what the point is?"

"Point?"

"Yeah," he said leadenly. "Point."

Defending the helpless and hopeless was not piece of cake on a day-in day-out basis. So many of his clients were petty, small-time losers. No sooner were they off the hook, if they were that lucky, than they were back doing what got them in trouble in the first place. Each day he rolled the boulder up the hill, each night it toppled back down. And no one really gave a damn.

"You need a vacation."

"Let's go somewhere, then."

"Why did you want to know if I knew a Jim Walker?"

43

"Who? Oh that. Just a phone message I had to call a guy. Said he knew you."

"Yeah?"

"Never got an answer. Never talked to him."

We stopped to turn around. We'd walked beyond the lights of the condos, halfway to the inlet. It had to be after midnight. It felt strange and sweet to be alone in the dark with him again.

He let go of my hand and started out ahead of me. I trotted to catch up. He was walking fast now. I tried to put my arm through his, but he wouldn't let me.

"You need to quit that job, Chester."

"Who's Jim Walker?"

"A student of mine."

"That's it?"

"Well, no. He helped me get my car out of a ditch and then disappeared with it."

Behind us, the ground had begun to shake. The thudding, rhythmic steps of a runner. I turned to look. Out of the mist, a shirtless barrel-chested man in long pants was gradually emerging. I took Chester's arm. He looked over his shoulder. The man passed us without looking at us. A chill ran through me. He'd come so close, I could have touched his perspiring shoulders.

"It's him. It's the guy." Chester sprang to go after him, but I grabbed his shirt.

"Please, don't. Don't!"

The man jogged off into the dark and then vanished. The last I saw of him was the jiggling spare tire around his middle. Ringo caught up with us just as the man disappeared. Sopping wet, covered with sand, tongue hanging out, idiotically dog-happy.

Chester called Lance at home from my place. A couple of squad cars were sent down to the beach to see if they could pick up the trail, but Lance was doubtful. For a few moments Chester drummed his fingers on my kitchen table and stared off into space. Then he kicked off his shoes and stretched out on my couch fully clothed, looking cramped and grumpy, with Ring on the floor next to him. "Thanks," I said from the foot of the stairs. Everything with us was so damn complicated.

✛ ✛ ✛

In the morning he was gone. No note, nothing. Par for the course, but I was irritated anyway.

The other man in my life that I cared to think about had also abandoned me. I tried to reach Randy at the *Herald* but they said he was out on assignment. They put me through to his editor when I pressed for details.

"He's in Homestead for the day."

"Doing what?"

"Are you the stringer we took on up there? What's your name again? Ruby something?"

"My invoices say Garnet Sullivan."

"So what's happening up there?"

"I need to talk to Randy ASAP." *Never trust an Editor*, the first rule of freelancing.

"Like I said, he's out. What can I do for you? You have anything to file?"

"I might. Have Randy call me, please."

I supposed that Homestead meant Mossbach Nurseries and Randy had gone down there to sniff around Julie's boyfriend's lair. I wondered if he'd been in touch with the kids yet and had an itch to chat them up myself.

I fixed myself a cup of orange zinger and went out to my patio. My neighbor's yellow cat was sunning himself on my lounge chair. I sat down next to him and he tucked in his toes and purred.

What is it about some men and sharks? An elemental fascination exists there. David Devaigne was only an extreme case. Go out in a big boat with whopping tackle, a bunch of dope and pornographic magazines. Get high, get aroused and fish like hell for the monster of the deep. This was a guy who pushed things to the red limit. Someone who thought the rules applied to everyone but himself.

"What do you think, Larry?" The cat yawned and stretched, hopped down and wandered off with his tail in the air. An ugly anvil-shaped cloud was forming to the west, across the river.

Now Fendermann, he was a conventional kind of a guy. Riverside Drive address. A huge white Mediterranean villa with a beautiful blue tile roof on the water. Belonged to the right clubs. I didn't know him personally, but we had a few mutual friends. As the only Chevy-Cadillac dealer in town, he made waves. If Bunny and Jim knew he was having trouble, everyone at his dealership knew.

The things I could do if I had my car back.

✠ ✠ ✠

The rain came down in sheets and it looked as if it would pour all night. The taxi's wipers were worn out and all I could see from the backseat was a gray blur. We plowed through fender-high water in some low places that threatened to put us afloat. Around one corner, we hydroplaned into someone's front yard and out their neighbor's driveway. And for this death-defying act I was paying $40 one-way to the IRK-U campus. Deduct that from the $544 I got a month for instructing my scholars and I'd soon be paying them.

Assembled together and irate about having to be there at all on a night like this, we looked damply homicidal. The three hours loomed before us like a watery grave. I didn't dare take roll. I looked out into the faces of these folk who had worked all day at a job, probably hastily fed their kids and passed them off to a relative or baby-sitter, and then dragged their butts through the rain to sit in my presence, all in the hopes of one day bettering themselves.

"Take out some paper and a pen. We're going to have some fun."

A hand went up in the back of the room. "Is this for credit?"

"Yes, it's for credit."

"Do we have to use a pen?"

"Do you need a pen, Tammy? Here, use mine."

F-I-S-H. I wrote it in block letters in the middle of the green board with yellow chalk.

I turned around. Blank faces everywhere. I cleared my throat. "I want you to pick a fish, the most interesting fish you can think of, and tell me about it. Tell me everything you know about it. How it makes you feel. What it tastes like, smells like, acts like, reminds you of. How you learned about it. What it's good for. How you catch it, what it brings at market, what it eats, where it is found."

A sea of groans.

"I want you to write everything that occurs to you as it comes to mind. Don't worry about organization."

"What?"

"When you're finished, go back to the beginning and write the thesis sentence."

Undulating sighs and shuffling feet.

"You have one hour. If you have questions, raise your hand."

"What about porpoises and whales? They count? They're not really fish."

"Anything that swims in the ocean and looks like a fish, and that you fish for, counts."

✠ ✠ ✠

Fearing I'd made a terrible mistake, at the end of the hour, only two students still writing, the rest having dropped off their essays while refusing to make eye contact, Jim Walker materialized in the doorway. Disheveled and uncertain on his feet.

"It's outside and full of gas. Keys are in it."

"What's going on, Jim?"

"I can't talk now. Did I miss anything tonight?"

"Call me at home tomorrow. I'm in the book."

"Will this count off?"

"Not if you'll tell me about it."

His blue shirttail flapped in the breeze as he left.

EIGHT

The flesh was swollen tight around it.

✠ ✠ ✠

My eyes lingered over the budding gardenia bush in the brass planter. I shouldn't have sprung for it at $18.99, but I did. Placed next to my sliding glass doors, just off the patio, it would get the warm afternoon sun. Over the next several days, the tight green buds would relax into thick white velvety flowers. And the air in my living room would become intoxicating. I would sit next to it at night and drink a glass of wine and inhale all I could of the essence of gardenia. I would put on piano and violin concertos and just breathe.

Two and a half days without a car can wreak havoc with a routine. Not only did I buy a gardenia bush at the grocery, but dog food, milk, bread, juice and other essentials. Then I went to the cleaners and post office and luxuriated in having four wheels under me by cruising around for a while. Drove by the marina, and yes, the *O, Julie!* still reigned supreme over all the other humble craft. The yellow tape was in place, just as we'd left it. I picked up a Miami paper at the airport: no Devaigne stories. Randy had said he might be back today so I went by the Palms, but his car wasn't there.

By admiring the gardenia bush, I was able to ignore the fish essays stacked next to a red pen on my kitchen table.

"Ringo! No!"

As I was mopping essence of Ringo off gardenia leaves with paper towels, the doorbell rang. I peered through the greenhouse window above the sink and saw Jim Walker standing outside with his hands in his pockets.

His face was tight like he had a pain somewhere. "Can't stay but a minute, Miz Sullivan." He pulled off his cap. "This is a nice place." He came into the foyer respectfully, as if he were entering a church.

"Sit down for a minute."

"Sorry to worry you over your car. But something came up. I couldn't help it."

"Like what came up?" I sat down across from him.

A muscle worked in his jaw and he balled up his hat. "Miz Sullivan, there are people in the world who are not good people. Know what I mean?"

"I suppose."

"Sometimes they come between you and what you know is the right thing to do and everything gets mixed up."

"Have you been stealing cars, Jim?" I hoped to knock the truth out of him before he got his momentum up on the lie he was trying to tell me.

"WHAT?" He was floored. "No! Where'd you ever get that idea?"

"What about breaking down cars for parts?"

"Hey! What's the matter with you?" He stood up.

"Jim, cars are being ripped off all over around here. I just thought you might know something. Had to ask." I smiled at him. "The reporter in me." I pointed to the couch. "Sit down. I'll be nice."

"I know what you're talking about. But I ain't done none of it."

"But you know people who have?"

"Naw, I didn't say I did."

"But you do."

Looking at the ceiling: "Know about 'em, yeah. A little."

"People you work with?"

That did it. "Where're you getting all these ideas?" He put his hat back on. "I came here to get my assignments, Miz Sullivan. Just tell me what I got to make up and I'll get out."

"Where were you with my car all that time? Sunday, Monday, Tuesday? What was going on?" He was a likable guy. What a shame. He represented a case of beer on a Saturday for Chester.

"You ain't happy with the shape your car is in?" An edge of fury in his voice. "Well, lemme tell you, you're dang lucky to have your car at all!" He was at the door.

"Wait, Jim. I'm not judging you."

The door frame trembled. I followed him outside in an apologetic jog. He started the car and gunned the motor.

"I am on your side, Jim. I want to help you, not make trouble for you." He put the car in gear and it jumped out of the parking space. Pulling out, he left a yard-long streak in the pavement.

✠ ✠ ✠

I was smoking too much. I'd bend over to pick up something and, on rising, I'd sound like a leaky tire. I'd open my mouth to speak and a bird-like warble would precede my words. The peculiar angry guilt and cockeyed rebelliousness of the smoker pervaded my waking hours like a low level hum from heavy gauge electric cable.

The kids' papers were separated into stacks homogenous to the fish discussed. None of the women had written about sharks.

The afternoon sun bathed the gardenia plant and Ringo, who was stretched out next to it. The place had become so warm that I'd turned on the A/C for the first time since November. As I reached for a paper, something moved in my peripheral vision beyond the sliding glass door. I walked over and pushed the drapes completely open. A blue jay perched on the top of the lounge chair and stared back at me. The sun was streaming in the window creating a sauna in that part of my living room. Ringo was comatose, his red coat shining as if it were on fire. The sunlight put a shine on the dark waxy leaves of the gardenia. A breeze fanned the bougainvillea outside against the wall. The air conditioning unit cut off with a clunk and all was quiet. It was so still you could almost hear the light soaking into the sandstone carpet.

"Sullivan." A hand on my shoulder.

I shrieked and fell back. "Damn you, Trigg!"

"I rang the doorbell. I saw your car and when you didn't answer I thought something was wrong."

"You didn't ring the doorbell. Don't tell me that."

"What's the matter with you? I did too."

✠ ✠ ✠

Riverfront General Hospital loomed whitely above us, the eight floors of the old wing standing frumpily in front of the twelve floors of the sleek new wing, a project completed last year after several years of community fundraising. A private non-profit hospital, it was a dying breed in the days of managed healthcare. Lush orange-red hibiscus nestled against the walls of the main entrance. We were at a busy junction with signs pointing in all directions: Emergency, Admissions, MRI, Oncology, Pediatrics. Not one of them, however, said *Morgue*.

Somewhere in that monument to civic pride a student of mine wheeled patients to and fro as an orderly. Somewhere in this hive of activity an old flame, an otorhinolaryngologist named Percy, examined his seriously stuffed-up patients. And others I knew worked at the hospital: nurses, doctors, lab techs. But no one I could summarily ask, with little prologue, to help me get in to see a dead body.

"This is really pushing it, Randy."

His insect-eye sunglasses mirrored the hospital buildings. "After what you did on the boat? This is nothing." He strode up the walk scowling and rigid with purpose. He wore respectable khaki pants, a long-sleeved button down collar shirt and a bland tie. A new dimension of Trigg existence to me.

In the center of the main lobby stood an elevated circular desk with an elderly pink lady behind it. The front of her pinafore was studded with bright service awards and pins of recognition. Champagne coif, peach lipstick, be-speckled. She was going to be trouble.

Randy nudged me into the firing line. Her eyes were swimmingly enlarged by her thick glasses. "I wonder if you can tell me. I've come to identify a body." The lobby was the large cog in the wheel that was the hospital. Hallways shot away from it in countless spokes.

"Is this a recent occurrence, miss?" Eyebrows pinched, removing her glasses.

"Beg your pardon?"

"Is the party only recently deceased?"

I turned to Randy. "Been about a week or so, hasn't it?" he said to me.

"Not quite a week. A week on Thursday."

She appeared shocked. "You don't say?" she said, her suspicious eyes raking our faces for evidence of malfeasance and dissimulation. A long boney finger ending in a perfectly manicured peach fingernail then flew out from under the desk and pointed away from her. Other hand poised on the phone as if to alert security, she said, "At the end of the hall take the elevator down to level BB. Check in at the desk."

The elevator was full when we got in. White coats, green surgery togs, R.N.'s in crisp white pant suits, techs in cheery color combos, grim-faced visitors holding flowers and gifts. A rosey-cheeked Candy Striper with a book and magazine cart blithely took up a lot of space. At every stop on the way down, some tumbled off. Ground level, Parking, Basement. Randy and I had the elevator to ourselves for the final plunge.

The doors opened and we faced an empty hallway devoid of color and detail. A gray tunnel of dim fluorescent light. The air was bitter with antiseptic and something musky and heavier underneath it, reminding me of the fetal pig I had to dissect in high school.

At the far end of the hall stood a simple gray steel desk, bare but for a phone on one corner.

Randy groaned. "This place is dead."

I walked around to the back of the desk and opened the top drawer. A hospital directory in laminated plastic. A bottle of white out. A pair of latex gloves.

Out of ideas, I picked up the phone. It rang on the other end and then a man's voice said thickly, "Louie, here. Whatcha need?"

"Yes, I'd like to speak to the person in charge of the morgue."

"That'd be me. What can I do ya for?"

"I've come to look at my uncle Dave." A freshet of perspiration sprang to my brow.

"Last name?"

"Devaigne, D-E-V-A-I-G-N-E."

"Be right there."

Randy and I leaned against the wall and waited, feeling swallowed by the nondescript grayness. "It's freezing in here," I observed as a dark mole-like little man scuttled into view.

Louie thrust a clipboard at me. "Sign here. Follow me. Only one allowed in at a time."

"You can go first, Gretchen," Trigg mumbled as we walked down the hallway behind Louie.

✠ ✠ ✠

Louie conducted me into a room that had a wall of what looked like big stainless steel post office boxes on it. He consulted something on his clipboard, walked up to the wall and slid one out. A large vague shape in an off white synthetic bag lay on a stainless steel slab. Louie deftly tugged a zipper-like device and pushed the bag away from a bloated gray face. The ground moved under my feet and the room swam. Something unusual happened in the area of my stomach and intestines.

"You all right?" he said, checking my reaction. "Few minutes alone?"

"Thanks." I was afraid I was going to throw up and ruin everything.

It was just a dull gray swollen face. Featureless. The mouth open as if in mid sentence. The skin didn't look like skin anymore, more like rubber. Thinning grayish brown hair was slicked back from the forehead. The blue eyes were gelled open, all glint of life extinguished. A dead fish had more expression.

Feeling hot and faint, I touched the seam of the bag. It ran from head to toe. This was a big man. A dead man, but still very big. But what the hell had I expected? I pulled the little tag down to the waist and slid the bag away a few more inches. The walls of the room gathered in closer and the floor rocked under my feet. More of the same kind of skin: coarse, tumid, engorged with water. The hair on the chest stood out from distended follicles. A sort of rope belt was around the middle, Robinson Crusoe-esque. The torso was gashed and slashed; it had been badly mistreated by the inlet jetties and who knew what else.

I leaned forward and stuck out my index finger to lift the bag farther away from the arms and shoulders. In my sweaty concentration, I nearly lost my balance and fell forward onto the disgusting corpse. My ears were ringing. Ugly, ugly hole where the right arm used to come out of the shoulder: blue tissue, white twisted sinew. The other arm stood out from the body, apelike. The ring finger on the left hand wore a gold wedding band. The flesh was swollen tight around it.

A knock on the door startled me.

Louie stuck his head in. "Your friend said to tell you your Aunt Julie is here."

NINE

Sheer black silk panty hose.

✠ ✠ ✠

The potency of beauty should never be underestimated. Its indirect ramifications are felt dumbly but profoundly in every facet of daily life. The postman leaves the parcel with postage due, rather than the irritating little envelope. Dover sole is ordered all around rather than rib roast. A family moves to the Oregon coast rather than western Massachusetts. Generosities and grandeur bloom in unlikely places owing to a thrice removed relationship to a profile that was lovely in a particular light.

Louie, bolstered by the force of Julie Devaigne's classically beautiful face and sheer black silk panty hose, ushered everyone into the presence of the corpse, throwing rules and regulations out the window. It was a matter of conforming to divine will, the prevailing winds, and his own sense of utter worthlessness in the presence of a superior being from another, better world. He felt privileged to hold the door for her and barely stifled an impulse to throw himself at her feet as a runner between the threshold and the corpus delecti. He was a freak in abject servitude to a fairy princess with acrylic fingernail tips.

"Aunt Julie," I said warmly as she came through the door. "What a surprise!" *What a surprise!*

Randy brought up the rear with a face as blank, neutral and reflective as the moon. Whatever happened, he'd live to report it.

She wore the prettiest black silk suit with a semi-tux motif. Satin collars. White silk jewel neckline underneath. But it was nubby raw silk and so seemed just right for a Florida afternoon at the morgue. Perfect size six, if a bit full at the top. Randy wore an attentive blissed-out expression, suggesting he would have been pleased to pass the rest of his life cleaning her toilet.

She walked right up to the body as if it were a stand of fresh tomatoes. "Can you pull this thing down?" she asked Louie, pointing to the silly bag interfering with her inspection. Louie scampered into action, and in a New York minute the ambiguous remains of David K. Devaigne, tragically altered by time and circumstance, were laid bare.

I averted my eyes. Randy coughed. "Would it be too much trouble to turn him over?" she asked in a sweet, velvet voice.

"Not at all," said Louie. He nodded to Randy. "Get the shoulders, will ya?" he said as he grasped the feet. "On the count a three. One… Two… The body shifted slightly and rocked back and forth as the factotums prepared to execute the request. "THREE!"

With unanimous grunts, the two twirled the water-logged Mr. Devaigne into the air and he fell with a solid, non-buoyant thwack onto the gray cement, missing his slab by more than a foot. As he fell, the bag came loose, and the poor man was utterly exposed face down, on the cold impersonal floor. The flat cheeks of his derriere struck me as hapless and pathetic and indicative of the ignominious end awaiting us all. The grieving widow pursed her pouty luminous lips and knit her pretty brow. "No no no no …! It's okay! Just leave him there for a sec." She inched her diminutive black Amalfis toward her dead husband. With a tiny pointed toe she tapped the thick rope around Devaigne's waist. Then she walked around the corpse to the side devoid of an arm. Tossing her Judith Leiber alligator shoulder bag over her back, she put both hands on her cute little knees and leaned in for a closer look. "Tsk," she said. "Tsk."

Her lackeys Louie and Randy looked down, shame-faced, and shook their heads dolefully in agreement. Louie straightened his white coat and toyed with the topmost button. Randy smoothed the hair on the sides of his head with the palms of his hands.

Straightening, she turned to me with a frozen half-smile. "And who are you?" She had cold, cold blue eyes, glacial and impenetrable, fringed with expensive mink false eye-lashes.

"You mean you don't remember?" I replied gamely in a high girlish voice not my own (who was I, anyway?), my mind careening around blind corners and plowing through dark alleys of invention. I forced a helpless silly smile.

"Actually, no," she said, one hand on her hip, the other irritably flicking a bit of lint from her black bodice.

"It's me, Gretchen, Aunt Julie! Uncle Dave's niece from a previous marriage. His half-sister Mary's adopted child out of wedlock."

Trigg was coughing like a straining bicycle pump behind me. The vault containing the insulted body swung shut with a slow hiss.

"Well, I suppose we've never actually met, but I feel like I've known you forever! Aunt Mommy always spoke so highly of you!"

"What are you doing here?" she asked in a low, coarse voice.

I nailed Randy with a double barreled glare. "Randy and I stopped by to pay our respects. I live near here now."

I sidled over to Trigg who was obsessing over a hangnail, his chin buried in his tie.

Her sub-zero eyes froze us in place. "Him, I know," she exclaimed with a dismissive flip of her hand. And one and one makes two, right? "You're both reporters, aren't you?"

A sneer spread across Louie's face. "Reporters?" he asked, his voice heavy with disgust.

Embezzlers? Child Molesters? Serial Killers?

"What on earth? Reporters? *Reporters!*" I cried, stung. Who did she think she was talking to us like this? "I beg your pardon, you pompous prima donna!"

"Now wait a minute," Randy began, "This is a simple misunderstanding..."

"How rude!" was all I could think of to say. My parents were from the founding stock of Miami. My grandfather had a building named after him at the University of Florida. Great Great Aunt Sally led the charge to protect the alligator from extinction sixty years ago. This little bottom-feeding puffer fish had her nerve!

I wasn't really a reporter. Certainly not full time, anyway. I was primarily an educator... And a picaresque community activist ...

But she was on her way out the door. "My attorneys will be in touch with your paper," she said to Trigg, pausing in the doorway. "There are laws against imposters. Things like that." A tart cloud of Escada lingered in the air she had formerly occupied.

Randy, Louie and I filed out after her. Louie flipped the light as he went through the swinging door and I shot a goodbye look at Devaigne's holding tank. In the dim half-light, where he had only recently lain unceremoniously face down, a faint teal glow in the shape of his body, like a fairy dusting, rose up from the cement. Not unlike the sheen that had plagued my hands and forearms after my visit to the inner sanctum of his yacht.

✠ ✠ ✠

Trigg and I sat sweltering in his old Honda in the parking lot. Louie's threats and imprecations still rang in our ears. "Get outta heya before I call the cops!" being the most memorable.

"Why don't you get the air conditioning fixed in this piece of crap?"

"Did you see the look on her face when she recognized me?" Trigg asked dreamily.

Lady Julie knew the visage of Randy Trigg, staff reporter for the *Miami Herald*, like the back of her well buffed, manicured hand. He'd been dogging her physically and documentarily ever since Devaigne started eluding her divorce paper ensnarement, and long before he died. Most recently he'd popped up from behind a flat bed sod truck in Homestead as she and close friend Monty Mossbach were climbing into her Jag.

"Grass, grass and more grass," was the answer I got to my penetrating questions about what he found in Homestead. "And trucks, farm machinery."

"Do you think they had anything to do with Devaigne's drowning?"

"I'd find it hard to believe."

"Has she been seeing Mossbach for some time?"

"Sure looked like it."

"They grow anything else there but Bermuda and St. Augustine?"

"A few odds and ends. I saw some greenhouses. But his main line of work is sod for south Florida. His old man started the company a long time ago."

"How long can you keep a body on ice in Florida, Randy?"

"I have no idea," he said, starting the car. "Can't be indefinitely."

✠ ✠ ✠

There it was in black and white on the single sheet of sheriff department PR letterhead. A neat stack sat on the counter of the reception desk in front of the sergeant on duty for anyone who cared to know. "Asphyxia due to drowning, alcohol-drug intake and blunt-force traumatic injuries." The report did not determine how Devaigne drowned or was injured, but said "the injuries favor a non-accidental origin" and support the possibility of homocide. The sheriff department continued to investigate.

A clerk came out as we were reading and handed us a second release which said the body was being conveyed that afternoon to Miami for services and internment. Julie had won out over the kids in court and finally had her man.

Now it was up to Lance and the D.A. to determine whether a crime had been committed. The *O, Julie!* had put out at the inlet the first day of the marlin tournament, and that's where Devaigne's carcass had washed up. That was Lance's jurisdiction, although the Coast Guard covered crimes on the high seas. Maybe the two agencies would have to work together on this. And if drugs were involved in a major way, the FDLE or DEA might horn in. What a mess. Too many trees to bark up at one time.

I had to teach tomorrow night and had to have those fish essays graded and ready to discuss. I wondered if Jim Walker would cool off enough to return to class. I should call him and tell him about the writing exercise. It would be a way of making up.

"Sullivan," Trigg boomed, interrupting my guilt trip. "How well do you know this guy Lance Dawtry?"

"Follow me, Randy."

On the way down the hall to Lance's office, we passed an officer who had come to my aid when the man ambushed me at my door.

"We were just going to call you," he said. "We picked up a guy meeting your perp's description snooping around boats at the marina late last night. Sometime after you sighted him on the beach."

"You did?"

"Have a minute?"

Randy shot me an evil glance.

"Let me stop back by on my way out."

"Whatever you say. We're going to let him go, though, if you don't file a complaint before nine tonight."

Lance's desk was in no better shape than the last time I saw it. His organizational method seemed to be one of sedimentation. The important stuff was on top and the rest was buried history. We found him poking at the surface stratum with a letter opener, his face screwed up in concentration.

Finally he let go of a huge sigh and flopped back in his swivel chair. "Goldurn," he said, to no one in particular.

"Mind if we come in a minute?"

"Miz Sullivan. I hardly knew you without your bathrobe."

I introduced Randy to him and with little prologue asked him what the plans were for the Devaigne situation. He picked up the letter opener and went at the papers again.

"We've taken the matter under consideration. We're evaluating the evidence. Talking to folks. I'll have more for you in a few days." He carefully lifted the end of a dusty manila envelope with letter opener and looked beneath it.

"Like whom? Talking to what kind of people?"

"Family, friends. Business associates." With an irritated flick of the wrist he sent the envelope flying.

"Have you talked to Mrs. Devaigne yet, Lance?"

He folded his hands on the piles and leaned forward. "Well, Miz Sullivan, to tell you the truth, the idea has occurred to me. And I surely would if I could find her phone number. But something has become of it," he said, sweeping his hand across the wasteland of pulp in front of him.

"Let me know if it doesn't turn up. I might have it at home laying around somewhere."

"What about the rope around his waist, sheriff?" Randy suddenly blurted as if Newton's apple had just bounced off his pointed head. He had been silent up to that point, studying his notes and staring out the window.

"That doesn't look like something he would put on himself." Randy's cheeks turned as red as a stoplight.

"Right! And has anyone looked at the corpse recently in the dark?" I then said with a competitive thrill.

They both regarded me as if I were a two-headed toad.

"More to the point, has the body been released yet, Lance? If it's still here, you might want to have the coroner go over it with the lights out."

A goulish fascination lit Randy's face. Lance thought I was pulling his leg. But he wasn't sure.

"Now would that be by the dark of the moon or just the overhead lights, Miz Sullivan?"

Randy took my arm. "We gotta deadline and gotta run, sheriff. Thanks for your time."

On the way home Trigg berated me for holding out on him. It wasn't clear which annoyed him more, the eerie glow on the morgue floor or my possession of Julie's unlisted phone number.

64

For my own well-being and that of my chromosomes, I hoped the coroner would discover what gave off the pale blue-green shine and that it would be found harmless. I tried to take comfort from the fact that it had completely disappeared from my skin. For the life of me, though, I didn't know which solvent or lubricant finally did the trick.

It was a very peculiar color. The faded sheen a dolphin has just before it expires.

I was in a funny mood when Randy pulled up at my place. Not interested in how the story was going to be filed. Really didn't care to have any more input than giving him my notes. I told him if he needed me I'd be by my phone tonight and then said good-bye.

Once my eyes adjusted to the twilight of the condo, my spirits really hit the skids. Ringo had trashed the gardenia bush and dragged the remains around the living room, up the stairs, and stashed them under the bed. The remaining dirt in the pot he had flung all the way from the sliding glass door to the foyer.

Now he was spread eagled on the couch. He only raised his head when I came in. He was used to more attention.

At nine, after hours of cleaning, and as I was grading papers and listening to music, Randy called to get Julie Devaigne's phone number. While I was holding the yellow post-it and reading it to him, I remembered the officer from the hallway. And how he said they were going to let the suspect go if I hadn't I.D.'d him before nine.

Then another recollection bothered me more. I hadn't called Jim Walker.

TEN

A former Miss Florida.

I lay awake staring at the ceiling and the clock for an hour before I turned the light on. The jumps of the second hand failing to lull me back to sleep, I sat up, pummeled the pillow and surveyed the depressing evidence flung carelessly around the room. The unfinished essays were on my nightstand on top of a heap of unread magazines. When I sat up, Ringo slunk out of the room and helped himself to the water in the toilet bowl down the hall.

This was the kind of moment for which the phrase *the dead of the night* was coined. No question of who or what is there, for there's nothing there at all. I reached for the essays again with the anticipation of Marie Antoinette for the guillotine.

The writing was so bad, I wanted to throw up. But once I became numb to the poverty of expression and indifference to the basic rules of grammar, I became sensitive to themes, attitudes and feelings, and had to take heart. If nothing else, the essays were remarkable for the amount of fish trivia and old wives' tales packed into them. That's what you get when you ask people to expectorate everything they know about something. Nearly everyone had turned in five pages or more.

The fish were like counters in the sense that they allowed the writers to say as much about themselves as they did about their subject.

The girl that chose the starfish was a whimsical free spirit. The blowfish troubadour was a humorist. The lowly mullet received the methodic attention of an earnest plodding practical fellow. The chroniclers of the ways of the porpoise were happy romantics.

And these shark sorts. Their papers jumped and twitched with chest-pounding hyperbole. They brought to mind the crude routine of a barker for a run-down carnival. Some of their essays discussed the torture of sharks after they had been caught, though the writers would not have used that word. Gouging eyes out, pouring hydrochloric acid down their throats, nice stuff like that. A curiosity of this mindset, from a sport fisherman's point of view, was the length to which they would go to haul in their catch. The rules about line weight, tackle, only one angler touching the rod and reel, all of the telling details that made sport fishing a sport, fell by the wayside in the craze to land the shark.

I dropped the last graded paper onto the stack when the sky began to turn gray and went downstairs to make coffee. The local newspapers had run short notices about the coroner's finding on the front page. Strangely, they omitted any mention of the body being transported back to Miami. I switched on the TV just in time to hear a blond ditz say portentously that Sheriff Lance Dawtry would be holding a press conference at 11:00 this morning on the coroner's report and that additional information was expected at that time. Channel 5 would carry it live.

"Hope you're all caught up on your beauty sleep, Sullivan."

"I just heard. What do you think's going on?"

"The rope, that ultraviolet stuff. But Julie wouldn't talk to them."

"Julie what?"

"Mrs. Devaigne. I caught her at home late last night. Sort of patched things up. Dawtry had just tried to call her but she blew him off. Told him he'd have to go through her attorney."

"You're crossing the line, Randy."

"I know what I'm doing."

"What else did she say?"

"She knows all about the drugs and porno. Off the record said he was heading for a fall."

"Big deal. They lived together for six years."

"Said he had some unsavory friends and was not a very nice man."

"Did she also say the sky is often blue in Florida and that she expected the sun to come up today?"

"No, but she did say, off the record, that so many people hated his guts it was a toss up as to who did the dirty deed."

"I fail to see you made any real headway with your phone tryst, Trigg."

"She also said she wouldn't mind if I called her again."

"Why all the favors for the despised press?"

"She likes me, I guess."

✠ ✠ ✠

The press conference was held in a small meeting room off the main lobby. Mikes were set up on a desktop podium and camera crews had lights and boom mikes sticking out all over the place. This was a first for Lance as far as I knew. Nothing this newsworthy had ever transpired on his watch. The room hummed and buzzed with all the excitement of a county high school football awards banquet. Familiar faces from the backwater press lined the walls of the room. It was just like the big time.

I received several nudges in the ribs from peers who wanted to confirm the rumor that I was stringing for the Herald and that, in fact, the disheveled Ichabod Crane figure standing next to me was an actual staff reporter.

The buzz stopped when Lance strode into the room. He was dressed in a gray suit and crescents of white over his ears suggested a recent visit to the barber. The blue and red striped tie was a nice touch. His brown eyes radiated the wholesome intensity of a seventeen year-old quarterback. He fiddled with some papers on the podium, looked up at us and smiled. When he cleared his throat, we all leaned forward.

Reading from a brief prepared statement, he said that new evidence uncovered since the first coroner's report more clearly pointed to foul play in Devaigne's death and that the department was opening a full scale investigation under the assumption that Devaigne was murdered while in their jurisdiction. Then he folded his papers, smiled at us again, and started for the door.

"What kind of evidence?" Fred Phillips hollered from the back of the room. Fred was editor of the Stuart Times and my sometime employer. A C of C lunch regular and big community booster.

"No questions, Fred," Lance said. He pushed a boom mike out of his face to get to the door. A female Channel 5 type moved to block him. She held a mike in front of her mouth into which she spoke in low tones while blinking into a minicam. After a few agonizing moments, she held the mike out to Lance. "Excuse me," he said into it in a deep voice, ducking right and left. Refusing to budge, Miz Channel 5 then bathed the sheriff in a radiant toothy smile. Somebody in back shouted, "Butt out, Betsy! He said no questions!" Miss

Channel 5 scowled, but held her ground. Lance looked at her grimly as if he were wondering if he would be indicted if he just picked her up and moved her out of the way. Smelling blood, the rest of the press corps rushed the door.

"Who's the fox?" Trigg whispered in my ear.

"Nobody. She does radio remotes and weather. In her spare time sells ads for Thrifty Nickel."

Just as hell broke loose, thunder in the form of OKAY! roared out of Lance's mouth and the horde fell back. "Three questions. But take your seats. ONLY three questions and ONLY if you take your seats."

Amid the scuttling, I charged to the front and, after much shoving and elbowing, found myself under Lance's nose. I shot my hand up in front of his face.

"Miss Sullivan? You have a question?"

"Was the evidence connected to the body or the boat?"

"What was the question?" someone yelled behind me.

Lance fooled with the mike and it whanged and squeeled. Lowering his voice, he said, "Evidence found on both the body and the Devaigne yacht has led us to believe Mr. Devaigne was not alone on his yacht and that his death was assisted."

"Did you find any prints, Lance?" Fred Phillips whooped.

Lance's eyes found Fred in the melee. "Yes. We have some prints that are of a suspicious nature. Okay, one more question and then it's over." Arms waved in the air like so many lunatic octopi.

Then a horrible crash in the back of the room made everyone turn around. Chairs had been up-ended, camera tripods and flood lights overturned. Standing on top of a chair, victorious, was Randy Trigg, professional journalist. Head and shoulders above the fray, tie akimbo, hair mussed, indomitable.

His face disfigured by a blood-chilling warlock frown,

Randy tried to ask Lance a five-part question that was so convoluted no one could follow him and he got lost in it himself. He stabbed the air with his pen. Sputtered boilerplate liberal indignation and ended with barely concealed allegations of incompetence leveled at the Indian River County Sheriff's Department.

"I'm not sure I follow you," Lance said mildly. Randy was a curiosity beyond Lance's sphere of experience and beneath his contempt. "Next."

"Me! Me! Me!" Miss channel 5 shrieked, cantering to the front of the room with her microphone in front of her pink face. "There's a rumor going around about an alien substance, possibly toxic, that was found in the yacht and on the body. Is this true, sheriff?"

A startled expression took hold of Lance's handsome face and he bit his lip. "Well, I wouldn't call it 'alien.' "

"Then it's true!" Miss Channel 5 gasped, turning to face the camera.

"Hold it right there, Sheriff!" Trigg yelled hoarsely from the boondocks in the back of the room. "We're talking about biohazards here, this is a civil defense issue!"

At which Lance, head tucked in for the run for daylight, eyed the door being held open for him by two burly, uniformed deputies. "That's it, folks. There's nothing more to say at this point." He turned on his heel and marched out of the room, his face glowing like a hot coal.

✠ ✠ ✠

Trigg and I went over our notes and impressions in the hotel coffee shop across the street. He wanted to pursue the public health hazard angle, but I was of the opinion the starched shirts who ran Channel 5 would squelch the extraterrestrial motif that their dizzy representative was yammering about. We'd be in danger of losing our focus if we went off on that tangent. And after all, my hands and arms had cleared up. As the chief guinea pig for the operation, my views carried some weight.

"You could tell he wanted to cut and run," Trigg groused. "The guy's in over his head." Randy still smarted from being ignored. Lance's "next" would ring in his ears for many press conferences to come.

I blew on the fresh cup the waitress had just poured and stared out the window. The day had grown overcast and drizzly.

"This business about prints has got me thinking, Randy. Some of them on the boat could be mine."

"Probably are, Sullivan. But it's strictly circumstantial. The worst that could happen would be they'd nail you on a tampering with evidence charge."

"In a capital murder case." But how they'd ever find out the prints were mine escaped me.

Through the slithering rain a downcast trio approached the shop: Public Defender Chester Dare, bag lady Bettina Bassett and auto mechanic/night school student Jim Walker. Chester had on his old Burberry raincoat with the ink stains and carried some legal pads. The fog of a hangover shrouded his face.

"Lookee here."

"Howdee do, Miz Sullivan. Mr. *Miami Herald*." Chester motioned his companions over to a table in the corner. "I have been retained by one of your scholars, as you may have surmised, Miz Sullivan."

"Oh, no."

"Oh, yes. My two worthy clients over there have been arrested for stealing cars and dealing dope. Madame Bassett, furthermore, is alleged to be the mastermind of a countywide ring of car thieves and drug peddlers."

I laughed out loud.

"Due to his arraignment this afternoon, Mr. Walker is concerned he will be missing your class this evening. I have assured him you would understand."

"Oh, Chester," I moaned.

"It gets worse. Mr. Walker is wanted for questioning in connection with the murder of a Mr. Devaigne. I believe you are familiar with the case?"

Trigg was hunched over the table ferret-faced. He was going to spring somewhere any minute. His eyes darted from left to right as if he were watching a mental ping pong match.

Chester's eyes fastened on me. "Runaway with me tonight, Garnet. We'll fly to the South of France and never look back."

"Let's go."

"I don't get it," Trigg said.

"It's a long, long story," Chester said sweetly.

"Not that, not that. If someone had been on the boat with him, other people would have had to know. Think about it."

"Why do they want to talk to Walker about Devaigne, Chester? He's just a poor dumb redneck."

"He moonlights as a marine mechanic. Did some work on Devaigne's yacht. Somebody at the inlet gas pumps saw him on the yacht with Devaigne the morning he went fishing."

"No shit," observed Trigg. Turning to me, "See, I told you so."

"Told me what? You haven't told me anything yet." I caught Chester' sleeve. "What about the old lady? You can't be serious. People don't get more lost."

"Who? Miss Florida of 1955? Wife of the late great Buster Bassett?"

"Where have I heard that name?"

"He founded Bassett Motors here in the early sixties."

"Which is now Fendermann Chevrolet-Cadillac."

"She's Fendermann's little old auntie. Bassett left him the dealership. They didn't have any kids of their own."

I glanced at the shabbily dressed senior citizen sitting next to Jim Walker across the room. "Grateful sort, Travis Fendermann."

ELEVEN

An interlocking grid.

✠ ✠ ✠

Clusters of cattle, interspersed with clots of palmettos, dotted the horizon. So far we had spotted a pygmy rattler, two armadillos and a red tailed hawk. Ringo had jumped at all of them. In his dreams he could not have imagined such a lark. He was covered with sand spurs, beggar lights and mud and Trigg and I were in similar shape. The saw grass had sliced a red cross-hatching on my legs and I deeply regretted wearing shorts. The air was so humid and thick, it felt like soup.

"I can't stand much more of this, Randy."

He held the binoculars up to his eyes once more and turned around 360 degrees. "Did you hear that?"

"It was a blue jay. Maybe a crow."

"It was a voice, a male voice."

"How far are we from the road?"

"Couple of miles."

We had followed Jim Walker out to the sticks and had lost him. He was released on his own recognizance this morning because they had no real evidence linking him to anything. Coincidence and intuition were all Lance had to go on. The fact that he had helped Devaigne with his boat, including helping him cast off the morning he died, did not link him to the murder. Nor did the fact that he had befriended Fendermann's sob-story old aunt make him a drug dealer and a car thief. His explanation of how he had felt sorry for her and had gotten to know her because she hung around the dealership begging for hand-outs only did him credit.

However, the fact that a sheriff's deputy stopped Bettina Bassett driving a stolen late-model BMW with a bale of marijuana in the backseat pretty much sealed her fate. She could not remember where she had gotten the car and claimed the grass in the backseat was hay.

Randy and I were to meet at HQ to quiz Lance about breaks. He and I drove up separately just as Bunny Knapp was pulling away from the curb with Walker in his Pontiac. Ever the opportunist, Trigg hopped in my car and insisted we tail them. I objected that this would make Ringo a no-show for his annual shots later this afternoon. Trigg didn't care.

We followed them several miles down US 1 to Ft. Pierce toward the turnpike. My hunch was that they would pick up the turnpike, but instead they flew right by it and swerved off onto a two-lane blacktop which went about thirty miles through orange groves and cattle pastures. Then, minus a turn signal and barely slowing, they cut left onto a one-lane gravel road that ran through an orange grove. The gravel road dead-ended at the dike of drainage canal. No sign of them anywhere. No tracks, not anything.

Randy and I had gotten out of my car at the dike and climbed up the embankment to get a better view. The canal was about twenty feet wide and part of an interlocking grid of canals that ran through orange groves and pastures. From the top of the embankment we could see dark lines of Australian pines stretching up and down the borders of the canals. At regular intervals were metal locks and turnstiles for regulating the water. Cattle grazed in the distance. On high, to the west of us, a buzzard soared on a thermal. From the same direction came a faint intermittent sound of a motor running and the clank of metal hitting metal.

With little more than a nod of agreement, we lit out after the noise. But two hours into our trek we had long since ceased hearing anything that was not obviously an indigenous life form to the area.

"This is ridiculous, Trigg. We don't know where we're going or what we're looking for. Let's head back." We'd be lucky to get back to the car before dark.

"Wait. Listen."

"I don't hear a darn thing and I'm beginning to think you're nuts. Let's go." Neither one of us had said aloud, *chop-shop.* I didn't kid myself that Trigg was bowing to my sensitivities. He was just afraid it'd be bad luck. He fantasized that we'd happen on it just as Walker was bragging to his partners how he had killed David Devaigne. Trigg's thoughts traveled along conspiracy grooves of massive proportions.

"That clutch of raggedy trees over there."

"That hammock? Forget it. I'm not going in there."

"Why not?"

"Because everything but people make a home in cypress hammocks. Squirmy, slithering, jumping things. Snakes, spiders, chiggers, deer, coons, skunks."

"Okay, hang loose. I'll just be a minute." He bounced out ahead of me like a hackney pony, lifting his feet daintily and rhythmically over the tall wiry grass in an impressive show of self-conscious, stylized valor. Ringo barked and whined to follow.

"Watch where you step, Randy!" Cow paddies and snakes were everywhere as were insects of such a size and heft that it would take a shotgun to bring them down.

Soon only the top of Randy's empty head was visible bobbing through the weeds. I considered going back to the car and turned around to see the way we'd come. The grass was parted in snaky waves behind us. We had zigged and zagged through miles of wasteland in pursuit of nothing more than a metallic whisper. A herd of cattle was edging across the path we had made. In a while they would trample it to smithereens, leaving no trace of the way back to my car.

I turned back in time to see the pink speck Randy had become disappear into the hammock. The sun was level with my face on the horizon behind some dingy clouds. When I moved, my clothes gripped my skin like wet cement.

I looked around for lighter knots and pieces of wood to fashion a dry place to sit. It was a trick to gather them up before Ringo took a whiz on them.

✠ ✠ ✠

The night before, Jim Walker had missed class. Chester called me late with a news bulletin. Walker was probably going to go free, but not until they had interrogated him into a wet noodle. Mrs. Bassett wasn't so lucky. Chester had questions about her mental competence. She was such an airhead he hinted he might get her off that way. She didn't even have a driver's license. No known address, no living relatives other than her nephew. Chester had called Fendermann to see if he'd post bail, provide moral support, or do anything. Fendermann said he was busy and would have to get back to him. Chester was still waiting on that call.

My class had gone reasonably well. The kids regaled one another by reading their essays aloud and critiquing them as a group. Some of them hammed up their delivery and were very funny. For the first time they really seemed to enjoy expressing themselves.

A few of the fish stories were wildly imaginative, though the authors swore they were based on fact. One girl insisted she had seen a mother porpoise flip her young into the air as they were born, "you know, spanking them to get them to breathe." A guy maintained that blow fish have teeth "just like people" and promised to bring one to class the next time to prove it.

And the things they claimed to have found inside sharks. Tires, jewelry, a tennis ball. The class macho-man Roy Yate said that he'd caught a shark just last week with a human hand and a TV remote in its stomach. This elicited groans all around, but he pounded his desk and said he was telling the truth. Said he'd taken the "whole mess," opened up shark, guts, hand and remote to the game warden in Indian River County. I tossed this away into my lead basket. The *Herald* gravy train would not go on forever.

Fat drops of rain pelted my forehead and arms. Lightning winked on the horizon. Still, no Randy. I stood up and saw the cattle had come much closer. They had obliterated the paths we'd made through the grass. Next to me, Ringo did his bird dog pointing bit. They were cracker cattle, a poor looking bunch, ratty, boney and every color imaginable. Now and then a gray Brahma-looking fellow with a hump and long droopy ears. Florida ranchers routinely breed their heifers to Brahma bulls to improve a herd's heat resistence.

As the dull-eyed, fly-scourged crew ambled across my line of sight, I became aware of an odd noise. WHAP, WHAP. It was coming from the midst of the cows. They turned to look at me. Vaguely curious, some few mildly cautious. I pinched the skin behind Ring's head to keep him still. For a moment, they all stopped, as did the whapping. Once they satisfied themselves that I was not a bull alligator or cowboy, they lava-like began to graze again and move on. The whapping resumed.

The sun was on the horizon and violet vied with salmon in a spectacular series of striped skirmishes in the gray clouds. The cows were fading into silhouettes, black against the fiery sky. Snorts and bawls erupted languorously from the herd as if they were a comfortable, if retarded, audience at evening's big show. With every step they took, the whapping grew closer. Near me passed a gray hump-backed cow with an enormous saucer-shaped foot. It was a foot stuck through a hubcap. Concave side down.

The bottom then fell out of the sky and the rain collapsed like a sand bag onto the earth. It was difficult to remain standing. Ringo cowered and whined as I spun around looking for Randy and any sign that might direct me back to the car.

Loud cracks, like firecrackers going off, came from the hammock. In the waning light, it had receded into a hillock-shaped black outline against the brilliant orange western sky. Then two large sand hill cranes took sudden flight away from it. Their long legs stretched like chopsticks against a salmon memory of the sun veiled by a drenching rain.

Under the circumstances, I had two options: stand there in the open and drown or head for the hammock. I put my head down, tightened my grip on Ring's leash and took a few steps. It was at least a half a mile away. The rain was coming down faster than the ground could absorb it and inches of water now lay on the surface of the muck, filling my running shoes. The lightning was coming closer and thunder followed the flashes within seconds. Now that the cows had moved on, Ringo and I were the highest points in the landscape. Florida is the lightning capital of the U.S. Floridians have a healthy respect for it. In fact, you have five hundred times the likelihood of being killed by lightning in Florida than you do of winning the lottery. I was terrified.

A bang like a cosmic crash sounded overhead. Ringo yelped and my ears rang like cymbals. I put my hand on his head to pull him close and saw that he'd lost control of himself. It broke my heart.

Then an itching sensation came over my scalp and I felt my hair lifting away from my head toward the sky. I knew what was happening. Happens hundreds of times a year in the sunshine state. Static electricity in my hair was providing the upstroke the lightning needed to connect with its downstroke to the earth. Wailing, I dropped to my knees in the muck and curled around Ringo as blinding light swallowed everything in a sheer white lunatic din. When I finally opened my eyes, I saw lightning had struck the small pile of wood I'd been sitting on just moments before and had plowed a six foot trench in the earth around it. I crossed myself. I guessed it wasn't my time, *alleluiah.*

Ring and I stayed flattened in the watery muck. The rain accelerated and drummed the landscape as if it would scour it clean of all detail and irregularity. Ringo writhed in my arms and uttered an unearthly howl. I pulled him closer and stroked his chest and the howl became a hiccupping sob, a lamentation so feral, I felt a sudden emotional union with him in our common terror.

✠ ✠ ✠

We reached the hammock as the last light left the sky. The rain had stopped, but water continued to pour from the drenched pines and cypress. The interlude of sinister quiet that had followed the storm was being displaced by the sounds of night life on the prairie. Sharp bird cries and rustling in the underbrush. I thought circling the hammock first, before plunging in, to be a sterling idea. We met a raccoon family on its way out for supper, two big dark shapes, followed by two smaller ones, scampering away from the trees into the night. Ringo lunged at them and scared the daylights out of me.

HELL! Someone then roared from the dead center of the dome-shaped, moss-flecked growth of trees. H-E-L-L! Ringo gargled something unintelligible in the recesses of his throat. A fragment from a poem about cypress trees by a Florida poet, whose name I couldn't remember, sprang to mind.

> *Now these mortified flagellants*
> *can beat their backs*
> *with their very own beards*
> *(complete with barbed mites),*
> *whichever way the wind blows,*
> *and never leave the kneeling position,*
> *hell becoming so familiar,*
> *hell becoming heaven.*

I knelt with my hands clamped around Ring's muzzle. Twigs broke, grass rustled. Something flew out of the top of a tree near us, hit the ground with a thump, righted itself, staggered off and took flight again. I got up and pushed Ringo into the trees ahead of me. Everything was sopping wet from the downpour and slick to the touch. I obsessed over coral snakes' preference for trees and branches until I recollected that Florida wild hogs had long sharp tusks and liked to root around trees at night as if they were discing it. I searched for wide swaths of overturned earth, and prepared to climb a tree if necessary, until a voice interrupted my panicky precautions.

"Who is it? Who's there?"

Was it possible? "Randy?"

I felt my way along slippery tree trucks and dripping Spanish moss toward the voice, and came upon a human form in a small clearing. He was standing next to a broad-shouldered cypress with his hands in the air.

"Trigg?"

Ring jumped against his chest and he swayed gracefully a few inches above the ground.

TWELVE

Not arrested, but insulted.

✠ ✠ ✠

We reached the road and my car about midnight. What finally saved us from spending the entire evening at the mercy of the nocturnal antics of Florida wildlife was the right-angled plat of the drainage canals. In the middle of my second tantrum, while I was holding on to Trigg's shirttail, he ran slap into a canal embankment. We agreed to follow the drainage canal and by luck chose an angle that dumped us out onto the gravel road where we'd left the car.

We rode home in silence, having exhausted most conversational topics of mutual interest in the previous twelve hours.

Discounting some of the embroidery to which his narrative style was prone, Randy was still lucky to get out of the hammock alive. He'd come up on a group of six men prying apart a Mercedes in the bay of a semi. The truck had been parked on the far side of the hammock from where we had parted. He'd tried to elude the men but two of them had run him down, pounded him with wrenches and hung him by his wrists from the branches of a cypress tree with a fan belt. The overhead lights in my car revealed a swollen black eye, cuts and bruises on his forehead and cheeks, and accounted for the new whistle when he spoke: the cap on one of his front teeth had been punched off.

The gang had high-tailed it during the thunderstorm, which explained why I hadn't heard anything. Trigg said he was certain that Jim Walker had been in the driver's seat in the cab during his showdown with the others and that Jim had piloted the truck out of the area.

The final bizarre twist was Randy's claim that he had spotted bales of grass in the back of the trailer, bales which shined in the dim light with the same gruesome blue-green gleam my hands and arms had registered after visiting the yacht and that Devaigne's corpse had left on the morgue floor.

When I asked him how he knew the bales were marijuana, he said, "You could get stoned just breathing the air in that trailer bay."

✠ ✠ ✠

Trigg's hero status earned him the attention of everyone remotely interested in crime in Indian River County and resulted in a heated tug of war for his story. Our first stop, at my insistence, was Riverfront General ER, where it happened to be a slow night. He received the undiluted compassion and ministrations of everyone hanging around, including that of a juicy student nurse who was in a swoon over what he had braved in the line of duty. Fortunately, or unfortunately as the case may be, for the press stud, his injuries were minor and after two hours of sympathy and antiseptic, he was released.

Because the incident could not be linked, except by our

intuition, to Devaigne's death, the *Herald* didn't want copy so much as reassurance that Trigg was still fit to continue in the news trenches. But everyone local was in a high dander to hear his story. An off-duty sheriff deputy, who was chasing the student nurse, overheard Trigg telling her of his exploits and with a phone call tipped off Lance. Directly, Sheriff Dawtry sent two detectives to the ER to impound Randy and his wounds for a debriefing.

On our way out we were met by two groggy news hounds who had ER plants and sources. To their chagrin, the detectives blew them off. As one of them was my erstwhile employer at the *Stuart Times*, I became engaged in a tense conflict of interests involving not just ethics, but the drab matter of a continued monetary relationship with Fred.

As he put it, "You owe me, Sullivan. The fat times with the big city paper won't last forever."

I promised him a story in the a.m., and followed the sheriff's cruiser, containing Randy in the backseat behind wire, to HQ.

I met Lance coming out the front door as Ringo and I were going in. As he held the door for me, his eyes widened and he doubled over in a belly laugh.

"Don't hurt yourself, Lance. What're you doing here at this hour? Couldn't get a date?"

"Looks as if you've had a big time on yours tonight. What, mud wrestling?"

"Oh, work, work, work. You know me." I went to brush by him, but he sobered and caught my arm.

"Yuk. You smell to high heaven. But tell me this, Miz Sullivan," he said with a straight face, "why is it that I've received an anonymous tip that your fingerprints are all over the cabin of Mr. Devaigne's yacht?"

"What?"

He gave me a slow cool appraisal. "Whut do you mean, 'whut?'"

"I mean what are you talking about?" The trouble I'd been in before paled next to the difficulties I faced now.

"I mean I want to get prints on you before you leave here tonight, Garnet." A sad expression came to his eyes.

"Sorry."

I was relieved in one sense. I hadn't lied to him.

"You still want to go to the South of France?"

"Aw, baby, just say the word." He exhaled deeply as if the impulse had originated in the soles of his feet.

"I need an attorney, friend. Know a good one?" I doubted he could drive.

"What's the matter? Where are you?" His stereo system was blasting. A woman's voice shrieked with laughter in the background. All hope for a quick resolution to the mix-up leaked away through the receiver.

"Never mind. I'll talk to you tomorrow." I hung up.

Lance was standing behind me. "What're we going to do with him?"

"I don't know." And I really didn't.

"I'm going to let you go home tonight, Garnet. But be back here tomorrow morning, eight sharp."

✠ ✠ ✠

The lights on the causeway, which I'd seen thousands of times, surely, had a poignancy I'd never observed before. So neatly placed in rows and at regular intervals. Shining through the night. Rain or storm. Always there when you needed them to show the way. As if life itself were organized and well-intentioned and sturdy with meaning and purpose. And safe places were always at hand, easy to find.

I had to carry Ringo inside. The message light on my machine flashed but I ignored it.

I stood under the shower for fifteen minutes and then pulled Ring in with me for another five. I don't know what I'd expected when I called Chester, but hadn't been surprised when he answered the phone slurring and grandiose. I wondered if in some broom closet of my mind I even knew he'd be out of it. Chester was a binger. He'd take it for just so long, then ka-pow, he went over the edge. I might not hear from him for a week.

✠ ✠ ✠

Who knew I'd been on the yacht but Randy Trigg? I fell asleep with this thought winding through my brain like a snake. In my dreams little animals and insects were underfoot and the ground shimmied and writhed. Toward morning, a big thing jumped out of a tree and landed at my feet. It stood upright and lunged at me. I woke myself up groaning.

Lance was bright and brisk and looked as if he'd gotten more rest than I had. An open box of donuts was on his desk.

"You don't want a lawyer present?" No goofing, all business.

"You know the situation, Lance."

"There are other lawyers to be had than Chester Dare."

I glanced over to the plain clothes detective sitting next to me. Lance had introduced to him to me as Joe Somebody.

"I wonder if Joe could leave us alone for a minute."

Lance nodded and Joe disappeared.

"Okay, speak."

88

"I'm just going to tell you the truth. You do with it whatever you want."

"I hate to see you incriminate yourself without the benefit of counsel, Garnet."

"Come on. I haven't done anything so terrible."

"You were on that yacht, there's no arguing that. So let's just put that aside for the moment. Next questions are, when were you on the yacht and what were you doing there?"

A nervous giggle pressed against the roof of my mouth and came out as a cross between a burp and a cough. "Excuse me." I took a deep breath. "I was on the yacht checking things out when it first came back from Daytona. It was late at night. I was looking for a story. That's it. There's nothing else."

"What'd you take?"

"Not a damn thing!"

"We've got a problem, Garnet, you and me." Lance got up and walked over, standing above me with his arms folded. "You see, there are only two sets of clear prints on that big old boat. Mr. Devaigne's and yours."

I stared at the wall. "So?"

"I presume you can explain where you were the morning Mr. Devaigne died."

"Randy Trigg was with me the night of my visit to the yacht. He'll back me up."

Lance stared at me.

"And that morning... The morning Devaigne was murdered or whatever... I must've have been preparing for my class. I taught that night." I could not believe he really thought I might be involved in this murder. The awful power of law enforcement and the crisp black and white of the law was chilling.

"Speaking of which, what the hell are you teaching your students?"

"What?"

"Whut? Whut! I'll tell you whut: we've got a warrant out to arrest that Walker again. He keeps turning up like a bad penny every time something happens around here."

So Randy had told them. I hadn't talked to him after the detectives shook him down last night. But of course. He had to. "I didn't think Randy could be sure it was Walker he saw last night," I said weakly.

"I'm going to let you go, Garnet," Lance said, his teeth popping against each other and spittle gathering to the side of his mouth. "But I suggest you come up with some airtight explanations for the questions I've raised."

I stood up on rubbery legs.

"AND stay out of the way of this investigation or we're going to put your tight little butt in jail. We have enough to do that right now, if I wanted to."

I sat back down. "I don't like your tone, Lance." Now that I knew I wasn't going to be arrested, I was suddenly insulted. "You and I both know I haven't done anything really wrong. The murder investigation had just opened. There was no murder anything when I went snooping around that boat."

"You have really complicated things for me, Garnet. I can't run this office as if the press has any special privileges here."

"I know that." Next year was an election year.

"You can't run around this county like it's some kind of personal playground. Like I'm your daddy."

"Oh, for heaven sake."

"You trespassed on a crime scene. That's breaking the law, if I have to spell it out for you. And I'm not the only one in this office who's aware of it."

"I don't know what I was thinking that night. It was a thoughtless, impulsive act. I just wanted to get some news. If I took advantage of you, forgive me."

"Let's hope the D.A. comes up with somebody they can charge, because if he doesn't, he'll want to prosecute somebody for something. Even if it's only criminal trespass and evidence tampering."

Because he was up for re-election too. "I said I was sorry, okay?"

"Just stay on your side of the fence from here on out. That's all I ask."

"Maybe I can help. Don't roll your eyes. Randy and I have some ideas."

"Such as?" He was leaning on the side of his desk. Interested, but not very. He popped part of a cake donut in his mouth and chewed. He could be so appealing. A wonder he was still loose in this cow town of determined, tough-minded, marrying women.

"It's sort of a unified theory. Everything's connected."

He picked up a nine iron that had been leaning against the wall and took a few short swings. "Go on."

✠ ✠ ✠

Mrs. Bassett sat on the lower bunk in the back of the cell, holding herself and humming and rocking back and forth. Two black women, one with long blond hair plaited in corn rows, were on the other side of the cell, lounging in their bunks.

The attendant, a skinny woman in high-water pants, unlocked the door and let me in. "Holler if you need me."

I sat down next to Bettina Bassett on the hard bunk and said hello. She looked at me and smiled, but kept humming and rocking. Chester had not been to see her in days and he certainly wouldn't be in today. Her bond was set at $75,000 and no one had come forward to help her post it. But then, she had nowhere to go, even if she did make bail.

"Can I get you anything, Mrs. Bassett? Toiletries? Maybe food?"

"Oh my," she said. "I can't imagine." She had a girlish voice, at odds with her down-and-out exterior. Chester said she had gone to FSU and had majored in dance. How had she danced through her life to this?

"Are you cold, Mrs. Bassett?" She was wearing a sleeveless sundress.

"No, no." High forehead, prominent cheekbones. Her skin fell in folds to her chin. I tried to picture her as the beauty she was so many years ago.

"Have you heard from Travis Fendermann?"

"Who?"

"Your nephew, Mr. Fendermann?"

"Oh no." She lay back on the bunk and scooted herself up so her head rested on the pillow. Then she closed her eyes.

I patted her hand and put my card in it. "Call me if you need anything."

I got up to call the attendant and the black women came up behind me. "That pore lady's sick," one whispered.

"Don't nobody want what she got," the other said. A little cry came out of the dark bunk.

"Her lipstick, Lawd, she been going on about her lipstick. All she want to talk about."

"Tell her I'll bring her some." I walked down the corridor into the sun, trying to concentrate on the story I had to write for Fred's paper.

THIRTEEN

You never know what you`ll find inside a shark.

✠ ✠ ✠

Randy Trigg was at the dentist and I was at my keyboard most of the afternoon. I filed a craftsman-like piece with the *Stuart Times* about Randy's brush with death and the chop shop on wheels. Then I queried Fred about the apocryphal remote and human hand said by Roy Yate to have been discovered in a shark offshore last week. Fred said go for it, so I was on the horn with the game warden and Roy for a while. Randy didn't want me doing anything more for the *Herald* until we could confer without the benefit of his rudely imparted whistle, so I had the time.

The game warden, Oliver Trotwell, was a friendly sort and flattered that someone in the press wanted to talk to him. He remembered Roy Yate clearly.

"Darndest thing," he said. "But you never know what you'll find inside a shark. They're the garbage cans of the ocean."

I wanted a photo, but Trotwell had sent the goods to the state game office in Tallahassee. He said the hand was in almost perfect condition and the remote was in its palm.

"It was a white man's right hand and had been severed at the wrist."

"How severed?"

"I couldn't be absolutely sure. The cut was pretty clean for a shark. It might have been made by something else."

"Like what?"

"A blade of some sort, maybe. But don't quote me on any of this. That's for the big man in Tallahassee to decide, you understand?"

"What kind of shark was it?"

"Big sucker, but average for its kind. A mako, about twelve foot, maybe nine hundred pounds. Roy had gutted it, so the weight we took here wasn't exact."

Trotwell said that makos are the most popular game fish sharks. "They'll put up a beaut of a fight and jump like the devil."

Roy Yate was in orbit that his fish story was going to make the paper. He volunteered for a photo with his rod and reel next to his boat, anything I wanted. Would I be interested in seeing his wall of fishing trophies? He even asked for a byline. "It *is* my story, Miss Sullivan, you know." I reminded him that I was the professional journalist. He accepted that, but then wanted to renegotiate his C.

The right hand coincidence was something to marvel at, certainly, but Devaigne didn't have a TV on his yacht or anything else I thought a remote would be useful for. And there was another problematic detail: his arm had been ripped off at the shoulder. After I finished the piece for Fred, I faxed off queries to other regional papers in the hopes of getting a run on it.

✚ ✚ ✚

Off and on, like a dull headache, the question of who snitched on me with Lance nagged at me throughout the day. Something in the back of my mind wanted to connect it to the man who had lunged at me from my oleander bush. After ruminating on it while I walked Ring on the beach, it occurred to me that my hunch derived from the fact that the man in the bushes had been watching me unobserved. Whoever told Lance I was on the yacht had to have been spying on me. I couldn't come up with a reason for Trigg to do it. He needed me too much. Although I wouldn't put that or anything else past him if it served his purposes.

But something bigger was eating at me. I had to get some guidance and relief on Chester. I used a spare hour late in the day to meet with someone who had been helpful to me in the past.

He went over the routine business about interventions, enabling, going to meetings. Of needing to get out of the way, of learning to let go. As he went through the litany, memories of my previous attempts to straighten things out unscrolled before me like an ancient text with a tragic ending. I watched the afternoon sun pour in the window next to us until it became so bright I stood up and drew the shades. And then I left. I must have said "I know" fifty times in fifty minutes.

✚ ✚ ✚

A mortified blowfish sat on my desk. It was stiff, dry, totally desiccated. In the puffed-up position. I picked it up by the tail. "Who's the wise guy?"

Tamal Freeman shouted, "Look at his teeth!" Tamal was not a fisherman, I knew, from his essay. He had written a movie review of "Save Willie" to fill the bill. No, Tamal was but a front man.

Obediently, I held the fish up and peered into its mouth. A puckered-up smooch and two very human-looking upper incisors. "I give. So it has humanoid teeth. I think I knew this. I've seen this a hundred times." I put the fish down and scanned the suspects.

George Furlong's face was buried in his textbook. "You win, George."

Weather permitting, I took roll. I was happy he was present, but something was odd about the way Jim Walker answered.

"Well, Bunny. Are you filling in tonight?"

She colored to her Clairol roots. "Yes, ma'am. Jimmy won't be coming for a while."

While the rest of the kids were working on their revisions, Bunny and I had a conference outside. I explained that though it was okay for her to audit and take notes for him, Jim would have to do the writing assignments himself. I also said that if Jim were going to be missing that many classes, it would be better for him to drop and start afresh another term. Bunny tensed at this.

"No, he don't want to do that. He needs this class to get his associate diploma. This is the second time he's taking it."

He'd lose the tuition money too if he dropped at this stage of the game. "Did he have a hard time with the work the first time around?"

"No, ma'am." Bunny squirmed. "He dropped. He took a night job at the marina."

"Doing what?"

"Working on a boat for someone. Engines and stuff."

"Where is Jim tonight? What's keeping him away?"

"He's out of town working at a job."

"Are you still the cashier at the Chevy-Cadillac dealership? How're things going there?"

"It's still kinda slow, you know. Things'll pick up, though. Mr. Fendermann's got an investor. Some guy kicked in money to keep us going till business bounces back."

I went over the fish story writing assignment with her and she took copious notes.

"Does it need to be typed?"

"Not this one."

"Because, you know, if it did, I could type it for him."

"Not necessary."

"Well, would it help his grade if it was typed?"

✠ ✠ ✠

With yet another bundle of papers to grade, I dragged myself home to decompress and ready myself for the next stint with Trigg. Increasingly I was finding myself in compromising positions with all of the interlocking relationships involved in my two lines of work. The latest being the fact that I knew Lance had a warrant out for Jim Walker. If I put some effort into it, I might be of some use to him in finding him.

A big white sheet of paper, folded in half, protruded from my doorjamb. A note from Allison Highsmith in her loopy handwriting. I had to call her and beg off. I just didn't have the time. But I knew once she had me on the line she'd wheedle another commitment out of me, so why bother? Find time. Make time.

I mentally composed a quick two or three graph release that would do the job just to get her off my back. Fresh air. Congenial people. Delicious Florida Seafood. All proceeds going to the Save the Manatee Foundation. It was to be held beachfront in an area that local surfers call the Shark Pit. It has always been called the Shark Pit and I didn't know what the true address was. A certain point south on A1A. I had to get the mileage from town.

"Ring?" Not a peep out of my roommate. I stood at the foot of the stairs. "Ring?"

Halfway up the stairs, my foot slipped and I caught myself on the banister. I looked down to find a puddle of semi-digested dog food. A large pool of the same unmistakable stuff was congealed at the top of the stairs. Way too much of my time was being devoted to canine waste and effluent.

I went from room to room. Okay, he was sick. But he wasn't here.

Yet he had to be somewhere.

After I had gone from door to door through the complex, all twenty-two units, asking if anyone had seen him and getting nothing but no for answers, and a few expressions of sympathy, I came back home, closed the door and let the tears come.

The recriminations that I had fended off for weeks broke through. I had neglected him. Left him alone too much. No animal can stand to be alone for long. Like kids, they act out. Then they get sick.

Then, while you're not paying attention, something bad happens to them.

Some of my neighbors had given me odd looks. It was only a dog, lady. Get a life.

✠ ✠ ✠

He wasn't dead on A1A and he wasn't on the beach.

With my flashlight, I walked the side streets that ran toward the river, taking routes we followed for his constitutionals. Pine Street, Shalimar Avenue, Shannon Avenue, Palm Court. Lights were going out in most homes. Flood lights were cut off, with a yard disappearing suddenly into the night, followed by the extinguishing of interior lights.

I swept the beam of my flashlight up and down the empty streets, around trees, through yards and bushes. A couple of cats slipping around, but no Ringo. I couldn't count the number of times we'd marched up and down those streets together. These same streets that he'd traveled when he kept following me home on my bicycle before I finally took him in.

On my walk back, after circling around about a mile's radius, I took a shortcut through a couple of backyards and the common area of the complex. Slipping behind a bougainvillea-covered wall, I came up the back way to my unit. The dark here was disorienting. Palm trees and the wall obliterated what help the street lights might have been. If I hadn't had the flashlight, I would have been lost. I came out of the trees and bushes to find all of the units dark, with mine alone shining in the downstairs living area.

I quietly turned off the light as I emerged from the bushes. Like the underside of a nightmare, he stood silhouetted at my sliding glass doors. White tee-shirt, brown pants, spare tire.

What did he want with me?

I stepped back into the foliage. He turned his head, straining to see through my curtains. Then he looked behind and all around him. The light cast from the sliding glass doors was enough: it was in fact the same buffoon I'd seen twice before at my door and at the beach.

He backed off from the door, walked out into the grass and paused for a moment. Then he started off in the direction of the clump of bushes where I stood. But he stopped and turned on his heel and looked at the glass doors once more. Crouching like a cat, he slipped around to the front of the building. I came out from behind the shrubs to the sound of my doorbell ringing. The three notes jangled, suspended in the hollow quiet of the empty townhouse.I walked around the building to the front. But he was gone. A large brown envelope lay on the doormat.

FOURTEEN

A twinkling gold incisor.

✤ ✤ ✤

The wind ripped through my hair and made it stand out behind me like a red hazard flag. With the top down, I could hear only an occasional emphatic syllable out of Trigg, although his mouth was flapping like a windsock. In a few miles we'd hit the cut-off to US 1 and head west from the turnpike toward Homestead.

It was difficult to smoke under the circumstances, but I was exhilarated to be alive. Ready to go wherever Trigg said we must.

What I thought was an envelope was actually a padded mailer. When I picked it up, internal alarms went off. It was heavy. Its weight was lopsided. I carried it over to Lance, unopened. "Wow," he said. "Good girl."

His bomb squad, which was ad hoc and under-utilized, sprang into action. They put on uniforms with goggles and helmets and amplified microphones. Consulted a huge ring bound manual. Then they were proud of themselves.

Uneventfully, they had unwrapped a dainty plastic explosive, rigged to go off if-and-when I pulled the red tab by the arrow.

I was afraid the man with the bomb had something to do with Ringo's disappearance, but Lance sensibly pointed out, "If he was going to kill you, why go to the trouble of stealing your dog?" Since Ringo was not trained to sniff out explosives, and few dogs are, he had me there.

I'd placed ads in all the papers offering a big reward. Called every vet in town, the pound in our county and the three surrounding counties. I even made a monetary overture to the people at the county dump, when I learned that animals killed on the highway usually ended up there. When I got back, if Ring was still gone, I planned to get him on a prayer network I'd heard about at a Catholic church. Before I left town, I forwarded my line to Allison who would field the Ringo calls while I was away.

Randy popped his first Miller Light at noon in Ft. Pierce. He had a few six packs iced down for the trip in a cooler. The pop tops and crushed cans were accumulating on the floor of the passenger side, with other papers and cast-off items, like a Sargasso sea. Dorito bags, Styrofoam cups, notebooks, newspapers, including the edition of the *Herald* which covered the Devaigne funeral at great length and with color photos.

Trigg was unhappy he didn't get to do the funeral piece. Some junior type caught the assignment. It was good luck, certainly, for a wannabee. The kind of piece editors and readers notice.

So now Julie loves Monty and Monty loves Julie and everyone knows about it, no more ducking and hiding. A little slip of a man, narrow-waisted with wedge-shaped shoulders and an out-dated blown-dry mullet haircut cut, Monty Mossbach was at Julie's arm throughout the whole trying ordeal. After private services at a liturgically conservative

Episcopalian church, David K.—which turned out to be *Klondike*—Devaigne had been cremated by Greater Broward Memorial Gardens. Then sifted and drained into an urn.

His kids had been photographed graveside for the internment of the ashes with stalwart vinegary faces. Julie's funeral entourage, with a smack of Hollywood about it, had stood off, away from the genuine genetic relations. Next to Julie's crowd, the kids looked like royalty. Modest, understated ensembles. Stoic semi-controlled grief. Their mother, Mrs. Devaigne, first edition, stood with them, a respectable looking woman in her late forties. The paper said she was an RN at Jackson Memorial.

Buried in the middle of the last four column inches was a pearl that I thought might have been worked into the lead. The kids had filed a brief, supported by depositions from expert witnesses, with the circuit court in Dade County only a month before daddy died, to have him declared mentally incompetent. The judge had sat on the kids' motion while Devaigne's attorney pulled together a rebuttal. The reporter had the wit to note that Julie's legal status under such a situation, since she had been suing him for divorce, was unclear.

It was a good article. The most exacting critic would have had to say as much. As a result, Randy was in his own personal hell.

When we pulled over at the Palm Beach service plaza I couldn't resist. "How do you think junior got wind of the insanity thing? That blows my mind." Not to mention what it did to the picture we were piecing together.

Randy silently unfolded himself and went inside. I sat and waited, observing a Latino family vigorously rearrange themselves in a black Chrysler minivan. Apropos of nothing, three crows sat atop the orange-shaped water tank and offered their commentary on the primate amusements below.

103

Poker-faced, Trigg settled back into the seat with his turbo snacks. "I knewall ahboot hit," he chewed, popcorn dribbling out of the side of his mouth.

Blood roared to my head. "You what?"

"I wuz thaving hit."

My view of my reflection in his sunglasses was not a calming one. "Saving it? For what?"

He took a deep swallow from a tall boy. Then burped ripely and gutturally, as the male of the species is wont to do. "The *coup de grace.*"

✠ ✠ ✠

The details of his Grand Scheme Randy kept to himself, but it was clear that junior's scoop had caught him off guard. Trigg had scored his own scoop by bribing a file clerk in the judge's office with fifty yard line UF-FSU tickets that he'd won in a raffle. He could only conclude that junior was at least his equal in finding the soft underbelly of good sources.

My association with Trigg and the *Herald* was losing its appeal with each passing mile marker. He regarded me as some sort of rude semi-civilized local scout, not as a professional peer. In his eyes, I was strictly adjunct and temporary. No point in letting me know the big picture. He called the shots. He dished out information on a need-to-know basis. And Pocahontas here didn't need to know nothin'.

Sated by fat, carbos and alcohol, feet poised on crumpled beer cans and snack bags, Trigg passed me a note. "We've got to turn up the heat on the Devaignes!"

I swerved into a "No Security" Rest Stop near the Boca Raton exit.

"Now what?" he said. "Want me to drive?"

The words strangled in my throat. "Out!" I finally yelled at the top of my lungs. "Get out of my car!"

"Oh," he said. "You're mad."

"You worm! How could you fail to tell me I wasn't the only one who thought that sucker was crazy!"

✠ ✠ ✠

On my way home, the image of an astounded, solitary, increasingly creeped-out Randy Trigg entertained and consoled me. He'd call somebody to come and get him, but Miami was a long way from the rest stop. He'd have plenty of time to consider his sins and view up close and personal the varied plumage of the *hoi poloi* that pulled into non-secured rest stops. If he had any cash on him, he would buy his way out of some nightmares not even a *Herald* reporter could imagine, uninitiated to the living breathing reality of deranged turnpike life forms. Or maybe he'd go native. Buy a gun and some drugs. File stories from the hinterland of madness. It was a career opportunity.

The *Herald* had paid me through the end of the month. We were only three days into the next billing period. Toke it up to experience. After things had cooled off, I'd call his editor and give him my side of the story. The situation could be finessed.

Pine trees, cattails, saw grass and culverts whipped by in a green blur. Clouds were mustering to the west, trying to get something going in the way of a thunderstorm. I sped onto a stretch of highway where all four lanes ran side by side, separated only by a narrow grass median with a drainage ditch.

A few trucks lumbered by, whining and snatching at their gears. At eighty MPH you've got to be fast perceptually, but I was sure that broken down semi with the red cones fore and aft had none other than Jim Walker standing by it. I'd swear to it.

I pumped the brake and shifted up. The truck had taken a muddy beating. Clots of mud hung from the wheel casings and made rooster tails on the sides of the trailer. I drove off to the shoulder and let the cars behind me pass by. When I got the room, I shot across the road, ambled through the depressed median, dodged my way across two lanes of demonically fast tracker trailers and pulled up behind the disabled truck.

The driver was now inside the cab, starting the engine. He turned on the blinker and headed back out on the highway, south. Without giving it much thought, I jumped into first and followed him.

He ran quickly through the gears and attained top speed on a quarter mile dip in the road. My speedometer read seventy-nine. The wind was buffeting my hair like an eggbeater. I stood on the gas and ran up close to the back end of the trailer. A Dade county commercial plate. Who would a trooper stop first in this game of high speed tag, him or me? I slowed to put some space between us and let a few cars pass. A camper with a kayak on top, a Jeep Wrangler full of kids, a truck hauling caskets from Georgia.

I passed Trigg wanly hitchhiking near a Miami Beach exit. In my rear-view mirror, I saw him vigorously giving me the finger and yearningly watch me disappear. May he hoof it all the way to Herald Plaza.

✠ ✠ ✠

The trailer was a drab unadorned white number. No identifying markings. Walker held his speed and passed several cars. He wasn't driving dangerously, but he was in a hurry. He was running with his lights on, and a short bleat of his horn preceded his passing maneuvers. The farther south we got, the more traffic we encountered. Soon it became difficult to stay with him. He disappeared into a convoy of empty fruit trucks and I lost him near Kendall.

I pulled over to a 7-Eleven just north of Homestead. Couldn't talk on the phone with the top down and somebody should know where I was.

"Put me through to Sheriff Dawtry, please." Walker was in this up to his nostrils. The longer he was on the loose, the longer his rap sheet would be.

"You weren't supposed to leave the county." Lance was miffed.

"Why not?"

"You were released on your own recognizance, but you're still in the loop, Garnet."

"I haven't been charged with anything."

"Come back here right now, or I'll throw the book at you."

"If I'm not home tomorrow night, send help."

"Not funny. I'll get a warrant on you if you're not in my office tomorrow morning."

"You're getting old, Lance."

I hung up and went inside to buy a coke. The cashier was behind a bullet-proof console.

"Could you direct me to Mossbach Nursery?" It was around here somewhere and probably was a big employer of the kind of clientele that frequented this store.

The man was shirtless and covered with black poodle hair. "Como?"

"En ingles, por favor."

Something then struck him as very funny. Gold incisor twinkling, he sounded like a car trying to start on a dead battery. A hirsute mitt shoved my change under the plexiglass and waved me off.

"Proximo!"

I stood in line at the pay phone for fifteen minutes to get a number but the phone book had been wrenched out of its binder and the empty cover dangled from the wires as if it had a broken neck.

While I was standing there, a fight broke out between two women and a man. They chased him around the parking lot until one latched onto a pant leg, bit him on the calf and brought him down. Then that one sat on his chest while the other one pounded him on the head with a shoe. The man screamed bloody murder. Nobody paid any attention.

FIFTEEN

Fingers frozen around a dream.

✠ ✠ ✠

I looked through the sheer curtain liner out onto the pool area littered with abused lounge chairs, fast-food wrappers and a woman's bathing suit turned inside-out. The room was rank with Lysol. No wonder the hotel had vacancies, but the price was right.

Allison had received several phone calls, she was glad to report, but none had panned out. "At least people are seeing the ads," she said. We were getting our share of crank calls and fake ransom demands, which took time and energy to sort through and determine that, no, they did not really have Ringo on a spit ready to barbeque, and no, the blue-tongued red Chow someone had found was not in fact an Irish Setter.

"I'm sorry to put you through all of this, Allison."

"No problem! I want to do this." In this instance, her good cheer was a boost. What a sport.

"Something's going to turn up, Garnet."

"Did you have time to put up those hand bills?" I gritted my teeth.

"Every shop and market on the beach. And a few in town."

I dialed Chester's number. He may have returned to the world of the living. I started leaving a message, but in mid-sentence he picked up.

"Speaking!" he shouted.

"What's up?"

"Can't talk. Where are you?"

"What's the rush?"

"I've got to meet Mrs. Bassett at the ER. They found her strung up in the tank with her pantyhose a few minutes ago."

"I'm at the Holiday Inn Express in Homestead."

If the old lady died all bets were off. One step forward, three steps back. The monotony alone was enough to drive me crazy. Already, before we even met, Chester's drinking habits and antics had cost him a marriage, a cushy partnership with a law firm in Vero Beach and untold financial difficulties, the full story to which even I was not privy. But here I was, hanging on, fingers frozen around a dream.

It was not the stress of the Public Defender's Office that was making Chester imbibe. I'd blamed it on that for too long. Something afflicted him on the cellular level.

I supposed I should have told him about following Jim Walker down here. But he'd hear about it soon enough.

✠ ✠ ✠

No one had ever tried to kill me before. When I considered it, it was an experience most people would never have. It made me ponder what qualified me for the distinction. Trigg and I had been onto something. Trigg! May he finish his journalistic career languishing on the Food Page.

The only reason I had for driving out to Mossbach Nursery was to see if that was where Jim Walker was headed with the truck. A semi-personal, quasi-professional curiosity, merely.

Small animals were coming out of the woods that bordered the two-lane blacktop into the evening dusk. I swerved to miss an armadillo. Out of the corner of my eye I saw a large wooden sign with green lettering and spotlights trained on it flash by: Mossbach Nursery.

Hurricane fencing topped with three strands of barbed wire surrounded the place. The large iron gate at the front was open.

Not much to look at. Heavy equipment: a few John Deere tractors, a Splundh back hoe, a Caterpillar bulldozer, two Bobcat forklifts, all parked neatly in open bays. Stands of empty wooden skids. A couple of dark run-down house trailers. A no-frills concrete block building that would pass for an office with some people in it moving around. In the distance, waves of quonset hut-shaped plastic greenhouses.

A roaring gush of water suddenly erupted all around me, nearly lifting me out of my seat. Huge rain bird sprinklers had come on in the outlying lots and kicked back and forth, spraying the sod beneath them. Miles of sprinklers swished and whacked in a deafening symphony of moisture. I pulled up behind a tall stack of skids and killed the engine.

Floodlights lit the four corners of the one-story office building. A white jeep, a blue pickup and a hunter green XJ6 were parked in front of it. Behind the office was a large, prefab metal outbuilding similar to an airplane hangar.

The lights from the office threw long shadows behind the skids, covering my car.

✠ ✠ ✠

The doors wouldn't budge. The building was larger than it had appeared. Must have twenty-foot ceilings. I made my way all around it in the dark, but it was sealed up tight.

Walking back in the direction of my car, the sudden appearance of a light in the middle of the night caught my eye. The overhead light in the Jag. Lotus-like, the car held a pretty woman in a shower of yellow light. It was none other than Julie Devaigne, checking her make-up. If she had been there all the time, she might have seen me when I came in. But maybe she'd just come out. She flicked her eyelids wide open with long red fingernails. After scouring her conjunctiva, she went to work on her nostrils. She had the full extent of her pinkie routed up her nose when the office door swung open and two men walked outside talking animatedly. Julie jumped and darned near gave herself a nosebleed.

The male voices grew louder and hotter. Monty Mossbach and a heavier guy, whose back was to me. Both had their hands on their hips and were shouting. I caught only an occasional word, but it was clear this was a conversation they would rather not have audited. Least of all by a sometime member of the working press.

Mossbach finally reared back like an egg-eyed agitated pony, raising himself up to his full height, and hurled "FIX IT!" at his sparring partner. That guy flung his arm out toward the rows of plastic greenhouses and shouted, "the damned plants!" Then he threw his arms in the air over his head and yelled "Fuck!" as he marched off to the pickup.

He trod with his head down and his hands balled up in fists at his chest like a boxer. Something in his walk, the sort of 45 degree angle he kept to the ground with his head down, was arresting. Haunting.

He tore open the door to the truck, jumped in and ground

the ignition. Hunched forward in the cab over the steering wheel, the lights from the office caught him full in the face and I knew.

What the hell was I doing here?

Another car door slammed and the Jag followed the pickup in a mad dash for the gate. Clouds of exhaust mixed with the light mist from the sea of sprinklers.

✠ ✠ ✠

I breathed slowly and calmly—the way they teach you in yoga class. When my heart rate slowed to a torpid one-eighty-five, I headed off on foot for the greenhouses to take a look at the damned plants.

As I was crossing the driveway, headlights swung over me and came to rest on the front of the office. Transfixed, I observed a wobbly Randy Trigg stumble out of a dented '89 Caprice, fork over some bills and turn to appraise his dark surroundings. The taxi drove slowly back out of the drive, leaving the weaving willowy figure silhouetted against the white cinderblocks.

The lights in the office were still blazing. Trigg stood at the front door and knocked. "Hi," I said into his ear from behind. "What brings you here?"

✠ ✠ ✠

On the face of it, locking up a plastic greenhouse was ridiculous. With Trigg standing by, I grabbed a wad of plastic in my hands and sank my teeth into it. It had the texture and consistency of an industrial-strength garbage bag. I handed Trigg a side of the slit I'd made and together we pulled in opposite directions. It was so natural.

Something about this man inspired me to acts of borderline lunacy.

Soon we had a gaping human-sized hole. He held it open for me.

"Your turn, Randy. I went first the last time."

With a sick expression, he slipped through the flap. Still protruding from the waist up, he observed weakly, "This is probably illegal, you know."

I nodded, "biting and entering," and gave him a shove.

The plastic swallowed him whole and he stood up on the other side. A muffled "wow" bounced against the thin synthetic walls.

On the other side he was a ghostly figure. Mumbles and exclamations sounded from him, but he made no more sense than he did ordinarily.

At last he returned to the opening we'd made, stuck his head out of the flap sideways, and said, "Un-BE-LIEV-able!" His hair and face shimmered in the dark, as if to italicize his announcement.

A veteran of a similar glossing, I began chasing him around on the outside, slapping my hands against the side of the greenhouse. It was like trying to catch a butterfly barehanded.

Winded, I returned to the tear we'd made and sat down. I might have tried once again to save some of his chromosomes, but I didn't. I found myself lost in a gripping reverie of tiny radioactive Triggs toddling around South Florida. Of how mother might keep track of them with a Geiger counter. The image suited the next generation of Floridians.

"Come in and look at these things, Sullivan," a shining head erupting from sheer plastic said to me.

"No thanks."

"It's grass."

"I thought it was supposed to be plants."

114

"They're GRASS PLANTS, woman!" he cackled, easing himself out of the flap. "Dope!"

He chuckled himself into a squatting position and slapped his knee. In the process he caught a glimpse of his gleaming blue-green hand in the dark.

"Oh no!" He extended his arm full length and opened his hand wide.

"You should see the rest of yourself, you little glow worm, you."

He slumped against a metal support pole. "Neutron Man," I observed, without malice. His shoes, hands and hair were brighter than the rest of him, but en toto gave the impression of a humanoid nova.

"Randy?" I prodded his leg with my foot. I was afraid he was going into shock. "Lighter fluid helped me."

The sound of tires on the drive made us look up. The blue pickup truck had returned and was racing up the driveway toward the office. When it stopped, Mossbach and the other man jumped out.

Mossbach went inside the office, but the other guy took off walking, making a beeline for where Trigg and I sat.

SIXTEEN

Rottweillers with macho cajones.

✠ ✠ ✠

The chemical storage tank was nearly one hundred feet long and had a diameter of twenty-five to thirty feet. It was low to the ground and supported by thick metal buttresses. Even in the dark, the word "Danger" emblazoned on its side in orange reflective paint at regular intervals was legible. Trigg and I were flattened underneath it.

"What's happening now?" Trigg asked from under the tarp I'd thrown over him.

"He's putting on a suit. Silvery overalls and a hooded jacket."

The man was donning some serious threads. Metallic gloves. A gas mask. He was just five yards from us, working out of a small shed adjacent to the first greenhouse in what were rows of identical structures.

Suddenly everything grew very quiet. The sprinklers had

cut off. The soft thud of foot beats became more pronounced. The man stopped at the end of the tank and made some adjustments to its gauges. His legs were foil stovepipes. A tinny clank sounded, followed by a protracted gurgle in the tank overhead. Then he walked off.

The door to the first greenhouse squeaked open. It was impossible to tell if he'd noticed the rip we had made.

"Wait here, Randy."

✠ ✠ ✠

The man had left the door ajar. As light on my feet as I could make myself, I hovered near the opening. The broad expanse of his silver back rose and fell in the interior. Serrated rows of small hemp plants receded to the vanishing point. Each sat in a basket of crenellated, withered leaves. It was as if the plants had risen phoenix-like out of their own ashes. They were an electric teal color and quivered.

The man paused at certain points, stooped toward the plants and twisted at an underlying metal scaffolding with a tool. He went out the back door and into the front door of the next structure. I slipped around the side as he would now be facing my direction and moving toward me.

"Hey, jerk!" someone shouted from the office.

I ducked back to my place next to Trigg under the tank. "You all right?" I whispered, poking him.

"JERK!" the voice cried again, more vehemently. Mossbach was standing in the drive with his hands cupped to his mouth like a bullhorn. Gathering his arms next to his sides, he began to jog toward the greenhouses. Something jingled in his hands.

I caught the phrase "yellow Volkswagen" like a piece of shrapnel. It was followed by the sharp noise of many feet finding traction and pounding off at a mad run on the shell drive.

They had my keys. Per my standard sloppy operating procedure, I'd left them in the car.

"We're history," Trigg said next to my elbow, a blue-green crescent of his face showing through the drapes of the tarp.

I socked him in the shoulder. "Stop it! You're always so damn negative!"

He curled up into a ball and said something about "dead meat." I popped him again harder.

"Hear that?" he said in a reedy voice.

"You mean those dogs? You're not afraid of dogs too, are you, you idiot?"

He pushed out from under the tank and stood upright, the tarp hanging around him like a tee-pee. "That's a lot of dogs, Sullivan."

A wild baying commotion was headed our way. Frenzied paws clawed up the marl and dirt, creating a white plume over the pack.

"Where did they come from?" Randy whined, clutching frantically at my sleeve.

"Come on!" I said, tugging at the tarp. "And keep that damn thing on."

We galloped over the dirt and grass heading for the heavy equipment bays. "Faster!" I yodeled out of the back of my head. Randy was lagging. The dogs were close enough now that we could hear teeth gnashing and idiosyncratic growls and snarls.

"Oh!" Randy screamed behind me. "Ohhh!"

With both legs pumping like an Olympic sprinter, I was still able to glance briefly over my shoulder. They had torn the tarp off of Randy and were ripping it to pieces. Gamely he was maintaining speed, abandoning the disguise to the teeth of the dogs, many of which paused to participate in its mad shredding.

Randy ran faster unadorned and soon we were side by side. Our new problem was that he now was visible to the naked eye for several miles as a result of his visit to the inner sanctum of the greenhouse. A few hundred yards separated us from the equipment bays.

Over the dogs' euphoric roar at the dying tarp, men's voices could be heard, shouting at them to get them back to business. Soon four maniacally scratching feet were behind us, then eight.

"Oh damn, run, Trigg!" A boom and a crack answered me.

"They're shooting at us, Sullivan!"

The dogs' panting was on the back of our legs. First one then the other snapped. Hot dog breath filled the air.

"Oh God!" Trigg shouted. "They hit me!" But he didn't slacken, he stayed with me.

Within a few yards of the bays, sharp teeth closed around my ankle. I kicked with the wallop of a mustang. A dog yelped and I lost my right shoe and sock. I slammed into a bulldozer, pulled myself up and grabbed Trigg under his arms. A black-eyed Rotty clamped him on the calf as I was dragging him up.

"Oh God Oh God.!" He screamed.

"Oh, shut the fuck up!"

He was such a baby!

The dog had his jaws locked onto his leg and refused to let go. One of those mastiff maneuvers, only dynamite would remove him. I pounded him on the head with my fists once more, more for vengeance than anything else, but it hurt Randy more than it did the dog.

I sat for a few seconds in the driver's seat gasping for air. Randy was slumped on the floor at my feet with the dog hanging from his leg as dead weight. I felt around for the key.

Except for the unusual gear shift and front-end loader levers, the thing drove a lot like a car. I put the pedal to the floor and we growled out of the bay. The front end loader groaned into the air before us like a shield. Skipping the drive altogether, I aimed straight for the gate.

When we reached the highway in a cloud of gravel and smoke, I didn't slow down.

✠ ✠ ✠

"Where're the lights on this thing?"

Trigg was wedged between my legs and feet. We were flying down the two-lane blacktop at full tilt. Dirt and sand flew up from the floor nearly blinding me.

Trigg moaned. The dog was still hanging on. I tapped its head with my toe and it writhed and growled. "Please! No!" Trigg begged.

This was going to be a serious problem.

Why weren't they chasing us yet? Of course they wouldn't call the cops. But why not try to take us out before we had a chance to get away?

Top speed on the dozer, burdened by two people of average weight and a large Rottweiler, seemed to be about 25 MPH. Neither Trigg nor I now had a car.

A Florida Trooper shot by us in the opposite direction without slowing. As long as Trigg kept his day-glo face on the floor of the cab, I guessed we looked okay.

✠ ✠ ✠

A chorus of insects cheered us on through the Everglades during the small hours of the morning. We passed a few farm

120

vehicles, but little else until we hit Pahokee on the southeast lip of Lake Okeechobee. Like a mirage, a green and silver BP Station rose up out of the murk.

They didn't get many dozers, particularly late at night, the attendant said. Particularly with a man so attached to a dog, he might have added, but didn't. I pulled into a full service diesel bay and with a wink asked him to clean the windshield.

The dog then sneezed violently but retained his grip on Randy's skinny pathetic calf. Randy yelped once, then went slack, burying his face on the floor of the dozer.

I felt the first tingles of compassion stirring in my breast. "I'm going to try something, Randy."

"No! Don't! Please, don't!"

"Shut up, Trigg, you damn wuss!"

I eased my hand under the dog's chest to its stomach. The instant I touched him, a noise like a spoon on a washboard came out of him. Randy screamed, mostly prophylactically. But once I got a good warm rub going, the dog's voice slipped up several octaves and elided into a puppy-like whine and simpering. His eyelids drooped and became heavy.

Before long, the jaw muscles loosened and soon after that Killer slipped like a sack of cotton balls to the ground.

I took twenty dollars out of Trigg's wallet, gave it to the attendant and told him he'd be a saint if he saw to getting him home.

✠ ✠ ✠

Randy sat on the floor of the dozer and held his injured leg the rest of the way. We didn't find any gunshot wounds on him, but he found a deep part in my hair where none had been before. Randy had some awesome puncture wounds, but I downplayed them. "You'll live, you pussy."

As we pulled onto the homestretch on state road 76 and drove east, the sky changed from a metallic twilight to a frothy cloud-specked pink. The vibration from the dozer had lulled Randy into a contorted slumber at my feet and had numbed me from the neck down. My every molecule yearned for a hot shower and sleep.

At the first intersection in town, a pickup full of sleepy construction workers on their way out for the day waved at us. I tipped my hand to my head, and drove on.

We passed Lance with a coffee cup to his lips, crossing the bridge headed into work. Though I felt unspeakably proud of myself driving this thing, I decided it would not be prudent to wave. He didn't see us. From the top of the bridge the sun was visible just above the horizon, a furious white-gold specter.

"Want me to drop you off at the Palms?"

Trigg shook his head wearily. He needed to go to the ER again, but I was not about to take him there thus powered. When we hit A1A and the beach, a squadron of pelicans flew over in formation and released some ordnance, scoring a direct runny hit on Randy's neck. He shook his fist at the sky and cursed.

Purring down A1A with the sun at a hot right angle to us, I thought I was hallucinating. What I saw sitting before my condo was an impossibility.

"Look!"

"At what?"

"What do you see over there?"

Trigg stood up. He turned his pained bloodshot eyes on me. "Isn't that your *car*?"

SEVENTEEN

The bomb boys.

✠ ✠ ✠

My townhouse smelled neglected and unlived in. A stultifying, disorienting quiet suffused the place, interrupted only by the fridge and a/c kicking on and off.

With Randy passed out on the living room rug, I scripted a speech and dialed Lance. I was woozy from no sleep and knew this put me at a distinct disadvantage.

"You're late," he groused.

"Lance, I would love to be in your office this morning. Believe me." I believed it. "But I would like to suggest that we meet over here at my place."

"What do you know about this severed hand and TV remote business?"

"What are you talking about?"

"You did a story on it for Fred's paper."

"Oh, that. Why?" Already the conversation had veered out of control.

"Yeah. Pretty weird, wasn't it?" Where was he going with this?

"Somebody from the *Miami Herald* called me about it."

"And?"

"Implied I wasn't doing my job. Wanted to know if it had been ruled out as part of Devaigne's missing member."

"Has it?"

"No. But it's highly unlikely, as I'm sure even you would agree."

My eyes sought the prostrate remains of my colleague.

"Who was it that called you from the *Herald*?"

"Your old buddy, there. What's his name? Prigg?"

"You're sure about that?"

"Yeah. Why?"

"Forget it."

Lance was amused that I was worried about the appearance of a white business envelope on the seat of my car. But after some schmoozing, I convinced him to come over with his bomb experts yet again. I held out the carrot of further info on Devaigne and the ring of car thieves and dopers, two things that remained distinct and unrelated to his way of thinking, but in which he was nevertheless intensely interested.

✠ ✠ ✠

With Trigg bundled into a taxi for a trip to the hospital, I raced around and cleaned up. I greeted Lance at the door fresh-faced with a UF Gator baseball cap cocked over my forehead.

The bomb boys conferred and then announced the entire complex would have to be evacuated. And off they huffed, knocking on doors and ringing doorbells, hassling everyone to hurry out, scaring everyone half out of their wits. Soon an odd assemblage of men, women and pets, in various stages of undress, huddled together on the asphalt.

"All right, folks, get back!" one of the bomb squad ordered, holding his arms out to his sides as if he were herding sheep. He marshaled the crowd over to the curb and stood with his feet spread apart in front of it. Mr. Bellini caught my eye and waved.

"Come on, little girl." Lance took me by the arm and led me over to his car. We would watch the exorcism of the Volkswagen from there.

"What if it blows up?"

"It won't."

With a smug expression, Lance threw his arm over the back of my seat proprietarily. When the guys gingerly opened the driver's door, he let it drop to my shoulders and drew it around me affectionately. A pastel cottony cloud of déjà vu descended the scene. I felt as if I were in high school again.

"I'm fine, Lance. I really am," I said, wiggling out from under his arm.

A muscle in his jaw contracted. The embrace segued into a boyish stretch and yawn.

"Have you picked up Jim Walker yet?"

Lance laughed. "Listen to you. Who do you think you are always giving me the third degree?"

"The reason I ask is that I have a source who says Walker is in fact connected to this Devaigne mess, but in an indirect way."

Lance sat up and fooled with his radio. "Who?"

"Can't say. But he's doing some kind of business with Julie Devaigne's boyfriend."

"Car business or dope business?"

"Maybe both."

He trained a skeptical eye on me. "Where were you last night? I tried to call you several times."

"Oh, I had my phone turned off. But I already told you. Homestead."

"Don't let's get crossways over this stuff, Garnet. We're both on thin ice."

"I'm not going to do anything to embarrass you."

The bomb boys had every door in my car open and the hood and trunk raised. One of them was looking our way. Lance motioned to him.

"What's the status?"

"Can't find anything." Then he pulled the envelope out of his pocket. They had opened it. "This seems to be harmless."

"And the envelope, puh-leese."

"Cut it out, Lance."

"What's that stuff? Hair?"

Three inch-long clippings of red hair had been inserted into the envelope in a fashion similar to the way they had hung from Ring's tail, a bright festoon that was one of the trademarks of a setter.

✠ ✠ ✠

The afternoon passed quickly and distantly somewhere beyond my bedroom walls. With the sheets over me and a death grip on a pillow, I tried to shut everything out and regain some sense of perspective. I turned off my cell. The ancient answering machine in my office was maxed out, but the phone continued to ring throughout the day, reminding me of how bad things were, yet, like me, the machine could take no more of it. Finally, after calling IRCC to cancel my class for the evening, I unplugged it and threw it in the garbage. Enough is enough.

I fell back into bed and listened as two mockingbirds outside my window sang to each other in full spring throat.

A breeze teased the palm fronds next to the building. The next thing I knew, Chester and I were walking barefoot on a sandy road together in a warm sunny place.

✠ ✠ ✠

Randy Trigg was standing at the front entrance of the hospital under the awning, legs athwart and hunched over on crutches when I pulled up. Over the phone he had told me he had his first rabies shot that afternoon and it wasn't all that bad. Not all it was cracked up to be. He had become something of an expert on the subject and wanted to hold forth on the different forms of rabies serum available and discuss his own particular bad luck at being allergic to duck eggs, because if he hadn't been he could have taken the dose orally instead of with the long needle in his abdomen. He sounded way over-medicated and much too jovial for his present circumstances.

"Let's go up and see Mrs. Bassett for a minute, Trigg."

"Fine! Let's go." He struck off at a brisk if unsteady gait back inside the lobby.

Short-circuiting Chester, I had called the hospital directly to inquire about Bettina Bassett's condition. "Fair," I was told. "Recovering." I had some lipstick in my pocket for her and had phoned in an order for flowers.

Randy whistled maniacally all the way to the eighth floor. When he wasn't whistling, he was smiling at the ceiling.

When the door opened at eight, he and I dodged back and forth trying to get out.

Exasperated, he thrust a crutch out the door and threw his weight after it, hurling himself into the chest of a man who was trying to board.

"Sorry!" Randy chirupped with a well-lubricated grin.

"Mr. Fendermann!"

Randy stood to one side smiling with drool sliding down his chin.

"Been to visit your aunt?"

He tried to place me. The last time I'd seen him was at a Chamber of Commerce breakfast more than a year ago.

I extended my hand. "Garnet Sullivan. I'm sure you don't remember."

But of course he did. I was the same chick who'd left hysterical messages on his voice mail on Sunday night about a lost car.

He looked at me blankly. "You're with the newspaper or something?"

"Sorry about Mrs. Bassett. That's really too bad."

"Yes, it is."

"But she's getting better?"

"Apparently," he said neutrally.

"I think two of your employees are students of mine at IRCC," I said in a flash of inspiration for small talk. "Or, one and a back-up for him. Jim Walker, one of your mechanics, and Bunny Knapp?"

He nodded gravely.

"Have you seen Jim lately?"

His eyes narrowed. "I don't get involved in the service end of my business very much, I'm afraid."

I lowered my voice. "I hear the police are looking for Jim."

"I didn't know that." Another whopper.

"I hope he's not in any kind of trouble."

Travis Fendermann checked his watch. "I certainly do too. Nice to see you again, Garnet."

Mrs. Bassett was propped up on pillows watching TV with the sound off. The lights in the room were dimmed and the reflected glare of the tube made shadows jump around on the white unadorned walls. Though it was a semi-private room, she was alone and the other bed had been stripped bare. She didn't acknowledge our knock, but when I walked into the room, she looked up.

"Hi there," I said cheerfully.

Randy lolled in the doorway and grinned. "Hiya." He waved a crutch.

A little smile flickered on her lips. Her eyes were glassy and floated from one thing to another. A dextrose IV was dripping into her arm. A budget-sized arrangement sat on the bedstand.

"Feeling better?" I couldn't help but notice she was hooked up to a catheter too.

"Catching up on the news?" Larry King in his madras suspenders huddled with a bald-faced lying member of the Jackson family pushing conspiracy theories. She might as well have been watching an infomercial on earthworms for all the interest it held for her.

Blue bruises flared from her neck, alternating with irregular crimson welts. Burst capillaries flowered on her cheeks and nose. She swallowed with effort and patted the sheets on her lap.

"I brought you something, Mrs. Bassett." She continued to pat her sheets, as if she were making a mud pie.

"Here." I put the lipstick on her lap.

She stopped patting and looked at it.

"I hope the color is all right. You have such beautiful skin. I tried to find a color that would bring it out."

"Put some on!" Randy said, patronizingly. "Let's have a look!"

"Dry up, Randy." I stroked her back. She was nothing but thin little bird bones. My eyes fell on the bouquet of pink tea roses next to us.

"Best wishes," the card said. "Chester Dare."

EIGHTEEN

Very tricky business.

✠ ✠ ✠

"Is this your Mom, Randy?" I asked, holding the eight by ten color photograph on the dresser.

"Yeah. Dear old Mom." He didn't look up from his notebooks.

"She's pretty." A mature brunette gazed tranquilly from the frame. Nice eyes and hair.

"Yeah," he sighed, "she was."

"Oh, sorry."

"It's okay. She's been dead a long time," he said clumsily. "I'm used to it."

Everything about Randy's digs at the Palms unnerved me. The room was too neat. All of his belongings were in tidy rows or stacks and lined up at right angles. There were no clothes on the floor. His few shirts hung in the closet at regularly spaced intervals.

And his desk area was especially annoying: a laptop, portable printer and tape recorder, all showing signs of heavy use, were carefully arranged for immediate employment. Off to one side, a well-thumbed dictionary and a falling apart *AP Handbook*.

He was a real person, not a cartoon. I feared the next thing I'd discover was that he had a really interesting hobby.

On the trip over from the hospital Randy had babbled enthusiastically about the great stories we were going to file. We were onto something big, very big. Unconcerned about his skin condition, he had so far ignored my pleas that he get to work getting the stuff off of him. I had stopped at a Minit Mart and purchased a large can of lighter fluid and a bottle of baby oil. The flagons sat untouched on the bureau.

He was slowing a tad. The whistling and grinning had ebbed. He rubbed and scratched his bandaged leg. "You use the sift-sort, pile and stack routine too," I observed. "I do the same thing."

"Is that right." He also obsessed over his notes the way I did, turning them over in all possible combinations.

"I need to call Allison and tell her about Ringo."

"There's the phone."

"Oh it can wait, I guess. At least I know who's got him."

"Yeah," he said vacantly.

"Randy!" I grabbed his shoulders and pulled him up. "Look at yourself, will you?" I pushed him to the mirror and switched off the lights. "This is not something to take lightly, friend!"

He hobbled in front of the dresser mirror in a blue-green haze.

"I didn't look that bad. You got a much heavier dose of whatever it was than I did."

"Guess so."

"Maybe we should tell someone about this. Go to the coroner. There may be some treatment you need."

"It'd blow our cover."

"Blow our cover? You look like a radioactive Tiny Tim!"

"Dawtry'd throw your butt in jail," he said, turning the light back on.

"I doubt he'd go that far."

"Not just yet, Sullivan." He sat back down on the edge of the bed. "Let's not over-react. This is going to make one hell of a story. We might be in line for prizes."

"Over-react!"

Someone next door banged on the wall.

"You're going to get me thrown out of here."

"What cover is there to blow? All the creeps involved know we're onto them." I grasped the bottle of baby oil and uncorked it.

"You surprise me, Sullivan," he said, harkening back to our earliest awkward moments together.

"Randy, they have my dog. How much more can I do?"

He shook his head, disgusted.

"I know what you want to do. You want to pre-empt the cops."

"Take a powder, Sullivan."

I pitched the bottle of baby oil at his head.

☩ ☩ ☩

The next morning I was at Chester's office before he was. Hazel Schmidt, his long-suffering secretary, opened up and let me in. Together we shared a cup of coffee and reminisced in the calm before the typhoon of Chester's office hours. Hazel told me she missed seeing me and wondered where I'd been. I cruised slowly around the room, browsing, and once stuck my head into Chester's private office. "It's a mess, I know," Hazel said.

A few losers dribbled in and sat down in the straight-backed chairs after signing in. They were depressing to look at so I searched for a magazine to read. Hazel chatted pleasantly with them as if they were paying customers. This struck me as very kind.

The public defender's office was one of the few government buildings in town where one could still smoke, so encouraged by the puffing of the other assorted dead-beats in attendance, I pulled out my cigarettes. They smiled at me collegially.

"What's that?" Chester thundered as he blew in the door. "A new 'do?'" He mussed my hair as he forged by his clients.

I followed him into his office. "Have a minute?"

"For you?" he said, flinging papers and files everywhere. He slammed the door and sat down behind his desk.

His mood was difficult to gauge. I wasn't sure how to play it. "That ficus needs some water."

"Ah. The plant patrol. I knew you were here on business." He stood up and walked over to a filing cabinet. "I have to be in court in fifteen minutes." He whistled softly.

"You look tired."

"I'm not." He turned his back to me and reached deeper into the filing cabinet. "State your business, Garnet."

Everything I could think of to say would only repel him. "I just wanted to see how you're doing. Kind of missed seeing you lately. Phone calls are great, but, oh, you know."

"How nice. I'm touched."

"So how are you? Been having any fun?"

"Oh some. Played golf with Lance the other day."

"Do any good?"

"Beat him." He laughed and rolled his eyes.

"I thought Lance was pretty good."

"He tell you that?"

"I wish you'd play with me some time."

He glanced at me over a file. "Yeah. We'll have to do that."

"I've gotten better."

133

"One would hope."

"Guess you're happy Mrs. Bassett pulled through. Those were nice flowers you sent her."

He paused and looked out the window. "Actually, her little prank saved us some time. We got a psychiatric evaluation out of it."

"That's good, isn't it?"

"Wish we could find Walker. He's connected to all of this somehow," he mused, reading a file.

"Ferndermann is too."

"Who?"

"You heard me."

"Is that what brought you here?"

"Partly, yes."

He put the file under his arm and came around the desk. "I'm not sure I like your hair that way," he said, giving me a platonic hug.

"It's temporary." I followed him to the door. "Good," he said. "See ya." And he breezed by the patient clods in the waiting room and walked out the front door.

✠ ✠ ✠

I went home, repaired to my office and powered up my laptop. As the screens unfurled on the monitor, the raw ends of my abrupt leave-takings with Trigg and Chester closed off and ceased to smart. I put the two of them in a 24-hour tickler file and went to work.

Preliminary searches on Google confirmed my suspicions. Genetic engineering, of course, was a huge and active field. Though scientists had been tinkering with it for decades, in the last five years it had gathered a massive head of steam and now had many accepted—even government endorsed—

practical applications. Recent citations unscrolled in dizzying numbers. I had to narrow my focus.

Gene and Marijuana
Marijuana cultivation and Genetic
Marijuana chromosomes and Cultivation

Too tight. For obvious reasons, I got no hits here. The sort of people involved in this were unlikely to brag about their breakthroughs. I tried what in my mind would be genetically similar plants. Corn, for instance. Wheat, other crops that the world had a stake in producing better varieties of and more cheaply. Now, mega data. All the big ag conglomerates predictably were streaking with it.

I had to rethink the problem. The glimpse I got of the interior of the greenhouse in Homestead was fleeting and imperfect. It had been dark and my raging adrenalin had interfered with the poised and open state of mind ideal for assimilating a new, as it were, life form.

Even so, the plants looked like miniatures. Bonzais of the original classic marijuana plant. And they sat in the cinders of what seemed to be a former larger state. As if they had experienced some kind of melt-down or implosion. Almost a culinary reduction from the inside out.

And they had a sick sheen that garden variety gene splicing wouldn't have produced.

The happy gardener in his space suit, safely sealed off from the greenhouse environment, had tampered and fiddled with a metal irrigation system that undergirded the plants.

Fertilizer and Gene

The screen convulsed and produced several citations about gene transfer from nitrogen-fixing bacteria to non-leguminous crop plants. All of them had to do with nutritional supplementation.

This wasn't exactly right. More than nutritional

supplementation was going on. The tiny plants seemed to have been bombed out of one state and to have evolved spontaneously into another.

Nuclear weapons and Chromosomes

A different mood swept across my screen as I scrolled through the citations. The sad chronicle of certain pockets of the Japanese gene pool after World War II. Soaring cancer rates and birth defects.

I quickly did another search:

Chernobyl and Chromosomes

This was more to the point and fairly current. A peacetime nuclear disaster from a power plant. But the citations were loaded in favor of news stories and short on scientific research. The few meaty sounding sources were in German and Russian.

I decided to take a blunt instrument to the problem. I picked up my cell and asked for a number for the University of Florida School of Agriculture.

I found what I needed in Dr. Greg Mendellsohn, an associate professor of botany on the fast track to tenure.

His work on genetically enhanced vegetables was cutting-edge and had landed him a large federal grant that the University was overjoyed to accommodate. In his own particular academic gene pool he was prepotent, a sire of several seminal studies.

"Very tricky," he said of genetic engineering utilizing radiation. "Difficult to calibrate." Powerful, yes. Years away from producing reliably repeatable results. Not to mention results safe for human consumption.

"Is anybody messing around with it, though?"

"Here? Only old Beidermeyer," he said, making a sound like a poorly strung voilin.

"What's so funny?"

Mendellsohn thought old Beidermeyer was a flake. Said

he'd been tenured so long ago, no one could remember how or why. Hadn't published anything in a quarter of a century.

"You should see the lettuce and celery he grows, though! What he claims to be doing is insinuating a radioactive isotope into certain amino acids … I don't really know the details," he trailed off. "It's fringe stuff."

Dr. Beidermeyer was in class at McCarty Hall when I called so I left my name and number, saying I was an admirer and wanted to talk to him about his work. The department secretary seemed surprised, but said she'd pass him the word.

Just for the heck of it, I typed in B-e-i-d-e-r-m-e-y-e-r on the Bowker *Books In Print* website. Zero hits. Nothing of his was in print in book form. Then I logged into Nexis. com and repeated the drill. Citations came up in *American Men and Women of Science* and *Marquis' Who's Who in America*. He was born in 1921 in Mainz, Germany. Trained at a polytechnic. Immigrated to the US in 1944. At UF since 1946. I ordered both complete documents and logged off.

✠ ✠ ✠

Nothing would come to mind to tell Allison about Ringo that wouldn't sound like a lie. I couldn't tell her the truth. Out of the question. When she recovered from her hysterics, the gossip would be all over town. The only prudent course of action would be to let her continue to believe he was lost and that I hadn't a clue where he might be. This would require some deft fakery.

To salve my conscience and get her to stop peppering my answering machine with cliches of strained optimism, I called her up and persuaded her to go to St. Mary's with me. Together we'd get Ring on the parish prayer network. It'd make both of us feel better.

When we entered the back of the dark church, she dug around in her purse and brought out her checkbook.

"What's that for?"

"Shhh! A donation."

"Then make it out to me."

Leaning on the baptismal font, she wrote out a check to St. Mary's for a hundred dollars and folded it in two. At the bottom she had written, "for Ringo."

"There. I'll tuck this in the box with the prayer request."

The trouble I was putting her through! It made me ill.

I picked up a little white form from the request box. "For Ringo's safe return to his home and family." I handed it to Allison. "How's that?"

Tears welled up in her eyes and her chin quivered. "Perfect! It won't be long, Garnet. I'm sure of it."

We went up to the altar and lit some candles in front of the statue of the Blessed Virgin. Allison threw herself down on her knees and buried her face in her hands. Every thirty seconds or so she shuddered and sighed. It was very distracting. I managed to crank out a few mechanical yet earnest Hail Marys. As I did, a sodden worthless feeling came over me. I pleaded with God not to punish my Irish Setter for my own shortcomings.

On our way out the door, I asked Allison if she wanted to stop for a drink, maybe get some dinner.

"Oooo, I'd love to," she said. "But I'm meeting Chester for a drink at the club. Lemme have a rain check, 'Kay?"

" 'Kay.'" It was a long drive home.

NINETEEN

Black cowboy boots.

✠ ✠ ✠

Other than the twiggy tentative foundations of an osprey nest on the microwave tower, the *O, Julie!* was unchanged. Moored in the same slip, trussed with the same yellow tape. Shadows from the afternoon sun threw into stark relief its elegant lines and majestic sweeping bow. I pulled into a marina parking space next to two cars from Orange County.

A peculiar aspect of the scene was that this beautiful ocean-going vessel had within it evidence of gut-busting perversion and violence. I was as aesthetically offended as much as anything else.

A cloud passed overhead and it became apparent that the lights were on in the cabin.

"Hello!" I yelled. The cabin door was propped open and plastic bags, instrument cases and a camera sat in a pile just inside.

A straw-haired fellow stuck his head out the door.

"Press," I said. "What's going on?"

He disappeared without a word. "Wait a minute!"

He reappeared at the cabin door and walked out, followed by a young Latino woman. Both were in civvies and held pliers and screw drivers.

The guy walked up to the bow. "Sorry. Off-limits. We're not authorized to talk to the press."

The woman smiled apologetically. "You better take off. A detective is around here somewhere."

"You guys from Orlando?"

They nodded.

"FDLE regional crime lab?"

The woman smiled.

"What's the blue-green stuff?"

They looked at each other. The guy opened and closed his pliers. "How'd you know about it?"

I looked around for the detective. "A tip. Know what it is yet?"

"Samples are still being analyzed."

"What're you taking apart in there?" A long piece of paneling lay outside the cabin on the foredeck, next to some black wires and small vents.

The guy's expression changed. "There he is. He's the one to talk to."

A Darth Vader character in a pair of black cowboy boots and an Orlando Magic ball cap moved toward me. Long hair, Hermes sunglasses. A new London Fog.

"And you are?"

"Little warm for that ensemble, isn't it?" He was in his mid-twenties at the most.

He rocked back on his heels, fists dug deep in his coat pockets. "This is a crime scene. Get lost."

"Press," I said pulling a smile.

"Let's see your credentials."

"Let's see your driver's license."

He stared and grimaced.

"I string for the *Herald* and some other papers. If you want to check me out, I'll give you some numbers to call."

"Somebody was just here from the *Herald*." His upper lip curled over his incisors in semi-contempt and stuck there.

"Who was it? A skinny guy on crutches?" Randy and I had to get things straight. Either I was in, or I was out.

"No." He looked me up and down.

"It's a big paper."

"A short fat bald guy." He produced a card. "Name of Lutz."

"Oh. Him."

"Yeah, so I already talked to the press. You can beat it now."

"Didn't catch your name."

"Nathaniel Lynch. L-y-n-c-h." He cracked a hint of a smile.

"I'm Garnet Sullivan, like it sounds. As you may or may not know, I've been on that yacht myself."

"One weird sonofabitch." He nodded toward the *O, Julie!*. "Some kinda fiend."

"You got that right."

Nate and I shared a cup of coffee in the harbor master's shop. He didn't know much, in spite of his tough guy act. The FDLE had gotten involved because of the quantities of drugs found. They had gotten a court order to seize the boat and, though Devaigne was dead, freeze the assets of his estate. This must have thrown Julie into a tail spin. What was she going to do for cash? The girl had parties to attend, a wardrobe to maintain, fingernails and facials to pay for.

But all of this Nate had told reporter Lutz. It only brought me up to speed.

"So what about the blue-green stuff they found on the body?"

He looked at me annoyed.

"Does this surprise you? I told you I was on that yacht just after it was towed back from Daytona."

141

"Mind if I smoke?"

"Are you old enough?"

We both lit up.

"The stuff was coming out of the air conditioning vents. Was hooked up to a canister in the anchor hold."

"What is it?"

He took a deep drag and closed his eyes. "It's some serious shit. I know that."

I wondered if Nate knew about the hand and the remote. Where that was in the jurisdictional and bureaucratic haggling that had been set in motion?

"Do you think Devaigne was murdered or what?"

"He was banged up and drugged stupid before he hit the water. Then who knows what happened?" Nate pushed his cuticles back and grew philosophic. "Me, I figure the scumbag got what he deserved. So, say somebody pushed him, beat him up? It's enough for an investigation, I guess. Waste of money, though. Good riddance."

"So you don't know."

"Don't care," he said with a crocodile smile.

Maybe they'd leave the murder part of the business with Lance and the county, after all.

"That bluish greenish stuff, it's going to take you places, Nate." I didn't want Randy to have all the fun.

Nate lit another cigarette.

"You smoke too much."

"You talk too much."

"Like you said, it's serious shit. Did you check out the grass on the yacht?"

"*Cannabis sativa x invicta*. High quality. Damned good stuff."

"Look at it in the dark sometime."

I let the hand and remote bit pass.

✣ ✣ ✣

I found Randy just where I'd left him. But instead of sitting on the bed, he was under the covers. The shades were drawn, clothes were all over the floor, and his notebooks sat in a undifferentiated heap on the desk. Empty bottles of baby oil and solvent lay on the bed stand. He said he felt like he had the flu.

"What else? You have a fever? Chills?"

"My hair hurts and comes out when I brush it."

"Let me see your hand, something's funny about your fingernails."

"The hospital called. They want me to come back. The X-rays they took of my leg yesterday didn't come out. They need to do it again."

"They probably couldn't find your bones. You're having some sort of reaction. You're going to look real funny without any hair and fingernails, Trigg. If you live."

"If I didn't know better, I'd think you were worried."

Toby Lutz from the *Herald* had been by Trigg said, without any obvious annoyance.

"The stupe's on vacation. On his own time."

"So let him look. But he'll stay out of my way if he knows what's good for him."

I straightened up his room, fluffed up the pillow and opened the shades. We ordered Chinese take-out. He wanted me to file a story with the *Herald* about the FDLE's involvement and include a few words on the hand and remote found in the shark. It was a long shot, but it beefed up the story.

"And check out the jurisdictional situation. How that might come down."

"Ten-four."

"And we need to get the details, maybe a legal opinion, on

the seizure of assets. What it does to all parties concerned, blah blah blah . . ."

"Roger."

"And call the kids, call Julie Devaigne. Get some quotes."

"Shut up, Randy. Go to sleep.

"I've got to go in for my rabies shot before five," he said. "Don't let me oversleep."

✠ ✠ ✠

On deck for that evening's fare in EH 101 was "Research Methods and Bibliography," the first of three units to be covered in class on the odious much dreaded subject of The Term Paper. Or "terminal" paper" as one pundit put it. Unattached to any specific research project, it was indeed deadly.

At break, I paused over the prize I was handed by Bunny Knapp at the beginning of class. Walker's better-late-than-never essay on a fish. Neatly typed with the words *Blue Marlin* in bold on the coversheet, it was a more polished effort than any other student had turned in.

Walker had cribbed from the encyclopedias and field guides. "Makaira Nigerians" was not likely to trip off Jim's tongue in casual conversation. I read on peevishly about "worldwide distribution in warm and temperate seas... highly valued by sport fishermen because of its size and the spectacular fight it puts up... Sought by commercial fishermen because of the fine quality of its meat." A pity he couldn't have been here tonight to hear my speech about plagiarism and giving credit where credit was due.

The middle of page two held a simple declarative sentence that made me pause. "The biggest marlins are always females." According to Walker's unattributed sources, males seldom weighed more than 300 pounds, and any marlin over this weight was "almost certainly" a female. Average weight for blue marlins caught in Florida waters was between 150 and 200 pounds.

The remaining paragraphs lapsed into Walker's own vague shuffling style and related his own personal anecdotes and observations. "Best marlin bait is bonito and tuna. Redder the better. Best kind of day is sunny and early morning." He made a few stabs at describing the tackle and gear and finished with a reference to the "oddest set-up" he ever saw. It was one he himself helped a man put together on a boat, a custom Hatteras. "An electronic trolling machine, like a winch."

"Very fancy," he said. "Rigged up to be operated by a remote."

"Bunny, I need to talk to Jim about his paper."

"Is something wrong with it?"

"I've just got a few questions. See if he can call me soon, will you?"

"He's pretty busy right now, but I'll tell him, yes, ma'am." She started off for her car, arms full of books and notebooks.

On my way back to my desk, I stopped in my tracks and called after her. But Bunny was out of earshot, and then was gone.

TWENTY

A curious aspect of the charges against her.

✠ ✠ ✠

The following afternoon I hung around my townhouse, dusting and airing things out. I'd put in a call to Chester after checking on Mrs. Bassett in the morning and finding she'd been discharged from the hospital—though not returned to jail. He was taking his sweet time responding, which came as no surprise given the way he acted at his office. Astounding how that man could put me on the defensive and make himself appear the injured party.

I was sure that the state had not dropped charges against Bettina Bassett. I suspected Chester had connived to have her stashed for safe keeping at a psychiatric crisis unit or some such place, trying to segue the suicide attempt into a full blown pre-existing psychosis.

A curious aspect of the charges against her was that they made her accusers look as crazy as she did.

If life were simple, I could just pick up the phone and ask Lance. But not anymore.

I'd been dithering with schemes to win back Ringo. But short of driving back to Homestead, I'd struck out. The notion of bait and fishing popped in and out of mind as a metaphor for a solution, but I couldn't connect it with any plan of action.

Randy had been lying low. He was in a funk with his editor because they held our story. "Not enough of a news hole. Not hot enough." We couldn't compete with the alleged cross-dressing of the mayor at a Santeria goat sacrifice in little Haiti.

"Relax, Randy. We'll be back on the board in no time." Although he hadn't said anything, Toby Lutz's arrival on the scene was an insulting development for him. His editor hadn't given him a heads up or anything.

"If something big doesn't break soon, they'll pull me off this thing."

As for our discoveries in Homestead, the editor was interested, but told Randy to "sit tight."

"What's he mean by that?"

"I don't know. I would have thought he'd jump on it. Something may be going on that I don't know about." *Ouch.*

Whether the editor had been plain about taking exception to some of our news gathering techniques or not, it was obvious to both of us that most of our information, from the very beginning, had been obtained by trespassing on private property, if not by some more serious infraction of the law. This would spell trouble in most reporter-editor relationships.

"Did he tell you to stay away from Mossbach's place?"

"No."

"Did he tell you to stay off the *O, Julie*?"

"No."

"So we're still okay."

"I guess."

After my chat with FDLE's Nate Lynch and what he said about the canister of gas in the anchor hold, Randy and I concluded Devaigne could not have been in A-1 tip top shape the morning he died. With that stuff pumping through the vents of the air conditioning system into the cabin, at the very least he must have been having the flu-like symptoms Randy was experiencing.

"You think Julie and Monty were trying to knock him off that way?"

"Mossbach? Yeah. Julie? No. She doesn't have it in her."

"Is there something in the air around here that is siphoning off male brain cells and replacing them with romantic vacuities, Randy?"

"Seriously. I don't have her pegged as a killer."

The night before, I'd gotten to him breathless with the news about the remote-operated trolling winch. Our bedazzlement with our well-aimed hunches soon gave way to a sense of our being grossly under-appreciated.

"So, you were right."

"We were right."

"And what's it get us?"

✠ ✠ ✠

I jumped across the living room for the phone, stubbing a bare toe on the vacuum cleaner, the same darn toe I'd broken a year ago chasing Chester on the beach.

A deep voice boomed through the line. "Docktor Beidermeyer here. Leeturning your call."

"Professor Beidermeyer! How good of you to call me back so soon!"

"Ya, ya. So vut can I do vor you, young voman?"

148

Praise if not sniveling flattery never hurt as prologue for a new source.

"I've heard the most amazing things about your vegetables. You know, your lettuce and celery? How big and nutritious... and... yummy... and, well, they're just fabulous, as everyone knows, and I'm working on a story for the *Herald* that I thought you, more than anyone else I could think of, would be able to provide some great expert opinion for, so..."

"Vut is dis 'yummy?'"

"Excuse me?"

" 'YUMMY!' Vut it is? I haf no time for nonsense."

The old prof was wholly immune to my charm and blandishments.

"Enough! Dis is leediculous. You are leediculous. I must go now."

"No! Wait! One thing, please! Just let me ask you this: has anyone ever used radiation or radioactive isotopes to improve marijuana yield?"

"Hurrumph! Vut is dis you say? Cannabis?"

"Yes, sir."

"Intelesting. Vy you ask dis?"

"I can't say." I knew right away I'd made a mistake.

"Ya, and the many things *I* cannot say!" Click. The old snot hung up on me.

✠ ✠ ✠

Frustration drove me out the door. I could not wait any longer for the calls that wouldn't come only to flub the ones that did. I could feel Beidermeyer's ears perk at the word "marijuana" all the way from Gainesville.

The birds were on their annual tare, flowers budded, jutted and thrust themselves into the sunlight. I put down the top on the bug and headed off in no particular direction. Driving helped me think.

I passed Trigg's flop house and found his Honda in the same place it was yesterday. A dog was asleep under it and it was covered with a haze of yellow pollen. Then I maundered up A1A by the beach for a short distance and took a left onto the causeway. Maybe I could ambush Chester at his office.

Cruising north on US 1, I happened by Fendermann's dealership. Something was changed about it. Brightly-hued triangular flags flapped in the breeze and amps blasted Garth Brooks' "Ropin' The Wind." Salesmen trailed window shoppers and browsers, their coat-tails flapping like vulture wings. WSHL was doing a remote.

"Miss Bunny! Don't you look cute today!" Inside her cubicle Bunny, in honor of the festivities, was dressed up like the Easter Rabbit. Ears, the works.

"Oh, hi, Miss Sullivan." Whiskers were glued to either side of her nose.

"What's going on?" I had to shout, because the radio announcer was grandiosely interviewing a couple who were absurdly happy about having signed a five-year note for a new car.

"All these new cars," Bunny said, "We've got a big new inventory."

"I guess business has improved."

"Yeah and," Bunny lowered her voice confidentially, "Mr. Fendermann's opening a Jag dealership too," she said, pointing over her shoulder, "next door. He bought that lot over there for it yesterday." She looked me in the eye. "Don't tell anybody yet. It's still a secret."

"Is Mr. Fendermann here today?"

"No, he left this morning to play golf in Scotland. He'll be gone for two weeks." She sighed. "But he deserves a vacation."

"Where's all the money coming from?"

"That investor, I guess. The one I told you about."

"And who is that?"

"I really don't know. At one time Mr. Devaigne was gonna kick in some cash, but I think that fell through. I heard Mr. Fendermann say he wanted too much control or something like that." She shook her head and her ears flopped. "I shouldn't have said that. I'm just a cashier."

Someone came up to settle a bill and Bunny went back to work. As we parted, she said she'd told Jim that I wanted to talk to him. "He said he would call you soon as he could."

"Translate that for me."

She shrugged. "I hardly get to talk to him myself anymore."

✠ ✠ ✠

I sat outside Chester's office in my car with the top up, trying to frame my approach. It was getting on in the afternoon. I'd parked next to his old Cadillac and had looked inside for clues to his present state of mind. A pair of air tanks and diving gear were jumbled together in the backseat. His pitching wedge and putter were on the floor in the front in a pool of loose golf balls. A Cuban cigar as big as a flashlight lay on the front seat.

When did he start smoking cigars?

I'd made a foray to the ABC liquor store at the end of the block. While I was filing a nail, the office door flew open and Hazel Schmidt bustled down the walk with her purse and an empty Tupperware container. She saw my car and waved, but hurried on without stopping.

After several minutes, the door opened again and an enormous white woman in flip-flops waddled out followed by a bean pole man in levis with a full white beard. A wad of keys jangled from his belt like sleigh bells.

I closed my eyes and breathed. I'd been staring at the door for so long that I could see it with my eyes shut.

Then something like a coconut or atom bomb hit the top of my car.

"What have we here?" Chester's live tan face said next to my window.

"Did you do that?"

"You mean *that?*" He whammed his open palm on my convertible top. "Or *that?*" and he brought two heavy open-handed thwacks down on the stunned roof.

"Some things never change," I said with a friendly snarl.

"Ain't it wonderful?"

"Hop in. Let's go for a drive."

"Nah. Don't have time."

"Don't have time for a cold one?"

His eyes flickered. He smiled the blazing white smile that made my knees weak.

"Get in, Chester."

TWENTY-ONE

The terminal stages of mirth.

✠ ✠ ✠

"'Roll on, thou deep and dark blue Ocean—roll!'"… Byron, if your memory failed you." I couldn't see his face. The sound of crunching ice followed.

His hand found the back of my neck and began to knead.

"'Ten thousand fleets sweep over thee in vain;

"'Man marks the earth with ruin—his control

"'Stops with the shore.'"

I slid a little beer around in my mouth. The tide was coming in and the sandpipers were nearing our feet.

"'He sinks,'" Chester bellowed, "'into thy depths with bubbling groan/Without a grave, unknell'd, uncoffin'd and,'" his voice became deeply sinister, "'unknooown…'"

We had nestled on a sea oats-covered dune for the rest of the afternoon like an old married couple. Cooler next to us, he swilled and I sipped until the sun dropped behind our backs.

"Okay," I said, trying to stand in the soft sand. "Time for us to roll."

Chester grabbed the cuff of my shorts. "Where to, Ophelia?" A full moon was coming up and shined like a flat silver dollar on the horizon. The wind off the ocean was warm and kindly.

I tugged at his hand. "Roll on with me, my deep and dark blue Chester. Roll!"

O Discipline! O Eye on the ball! I removed his hand from inside my pant leg.

"How's the cooler holding out?"

✠ ✠ ✠

By the time we left the turnpike and picked up I 75 near Wildwood, my friend was in the terminal stages of mirth. Rendered speechless by stomach spasms brought on by his version of my golf swing, Chester recovered with a refreshing slug of vodka. No sooner had he settled himself than he was guffawing to himself in the dark again.

"Okay! What is it?"

He held his sides. The plastic cup jostled between his knees.

"Something I said?"

This further convulsed him and he fell forward in the seatbelt. " 'Call this a govment! Why just look at it and see what it's like. Here's the law a-standing ready to take a man's son away from him—a man's own son, which he had had all the trouble and anxiety and all the expense of raising . . . Oh, yes, this is a wonderful govment, wonderful!'" He inhaled and hawed like a donkey.

Pap's drunken speech in *Huck Finn*. One of his all-time favorites.

"Speaking of govment, what's the govment going to do with Bettina Bassett?"

He strangled on a laugh. "Sheee's snot *crazy!* Sheeesnot!"

"No?"

He drummed the dashboard, deliriously, deep in a swamp of euphoria. "Nooo! Depressed! That's all, depressed!"

"So what's her excuse now?"

A wave of exhaustion crashed over me along with sour memories of my elliptical journey to Homestead with Trigg. The buzz from the one beer I'd sipped had worn off. I had become a chauffeur for lame brains and boozers.

"And!" he shouted, "I am about to cut the deal of a lifetime! A defense attorney's dream! Historical, that's what it is." He picked up my cigarettes and took one out.

"Hysterical?"

"His-TOR-ical! She's turning state's witness. I've all but got the charged against her dropped."

"Oh? And how's that? I mean, like, why?"

"Like, why do you want to know? Like, why are you so interested, little reporter girl?"

"She's a nice old lady, that's all. I'd hate to see her come to any harm."

"You're too smart for your own good." He began chewing his ice like a cud. "And you know why?"

"No! Why?"

"Because," running his fingers through the back of my hair, "you are forever hoisting yourself on your own petard."

"Cut it out."

"You may be wondering what a 'petard' is." He punched the lighter in and held a cigarette between his lips.

"I'm not."

"Then I won't tell you."

Two young does suddenly flew out of the dark and bounced across all four lanes of the interstate on spindly legs.

"See that?"

"A pe-tarrd is a trap you set for the other guy, but wind up hurting yourself with."

"So she's depressed? Who wouldn't be with all that she's been through? That Fendermann, he's in on it."

"I know."

"How do you know?"

"She told me."

I told him first.

"A pee-tard, Miz Sullivan. Think about it."

"And Walker?"

"The mechanic?"

"That's privileged information." The ash cratered and dusted the front of his shirt.

"So Mrs. Basset is only depressed. Wow."

"Aaand responding well to treatment."

"What are they giving her for it? Pills or something?"

Chester's eyes were at half-mast.

"So she's getting better. How about that."

"Well enough to finger a perp or two."

"And she's credible?"

"Miraculous change." His eyes slid shut and his head lolled on his shoulders like a crab trap floater.

✠ ✠ ✠

The sun was up when we reached the Newberry Road exit for Gainesville. Chester only stirred and smacked his lips. The streets were deserted and it hit me that not only was this an early hour, but the University might be on spring break. What if the old troll wasn't even here?

The campus was a ghost town. Not a stray all-nighter coming out of the library or a late night partier lurking in a bush anywhere. The carillon bells on the tower bonged out seven o'clock.

I headed for the ag buildings. Maybe Beidermeyer decided to stay home with his beloved vegetables. The tidiness and faux rural atmosphere of that part of the campus struck me as it had when I was a student. Always a stark contrast to the snake-haired pallor of the English Department.

I pulled into the McCarty Hall parking lot and parked next to a stand of knee-high corn. The engagement of the parking brake woke Chester up. His red eyes roamed from the corn to me to the corn. Then, as dignified as if he were entering a court room, he opened the door and got out. A few sea oats dangled from the back of his pants.

"Chester?" He strode off toward the entrance to the building.

He had been gone only a few minutes when the sound of meowing cats caught my attention. An elderly man in blue denim overalls with a cane was coming down the sidewalk. Two cats, a yellow tabby and a black and white number, rubbed against him, arching their backs. The man, who had a white Prince Valiant haircut, paid them no mind and they wound through his legs as he walked, yowling. As he came closer, a blue jay dive bombed his head in a noisy racket and he waved it off with a well-oiled, habitual fling of the arm.

"Ya, ya," the old man said to the cats as he drew nearer. "Voss is schloss?" He pointed to me and my car with his cane. "Und Volkswagen, mein kinder."

I almost fainted. "Professor Beidermeyer!"

He stopped. A trio of fat bumble bees floated in front of his face as if in a trance. He stooped to pick up one of the cats. "Und you war?"

I braced myself. "Garnet Sullivan."

"Ach," he groaned, setting the cat down. "I knew I vas not lid of you. Come mitt me. I vill show you sometink."

He wandered off ahead of me in a cloud of cats and bees down the sidewalk and past the corn field. We traipsed through a field of beans which gave out into an open area on which a large white plastic greenhouse stood. He paused at the door. "You like lettuce, ya? Eat your gleens?"

"Yes, sir."

He opened the greenhouse door and I walked up beside him. Inside were lettuces the size of beach balls. "My gosh. How do you do that?"

"Heh, heh." He motioned to me to follow him over to a wooden shed. He ducked inside and reemerged with a carrot as big as a fence post. He stood it on its end next to him. The tip came up to his shoulder.

"Holy mackerel."

"Nein. *Marlin*, mein nibblink." He walked off trailing the carrot on its side by its enormous green tassels.

"What?" I hurried to follow. He wound around at a tortoise pace through fields and sheds and after almost half an hour we finally came up to an out building that had seen better days. Its paint was peeling and a few of the windows had been broken. Beidermeyer pulled out a key attached to a long black ribbon.

"Is zimple. Blilliant und zimple. Zso." He opened the warped door which squeeked on rusty hinges. "I tell you. Vatch clozely."

The room was shrouded in cobwebs and dust. Something low to the ground scurried away from us into a disarray of papers on the floor as the door opened. A bird that had found its way into the building took flight from one of the many beakers on the counters, and began beating against the windows trying to get out. Beidermeyer left the door open for it and the cats slipped in behind us and began stalking it around the room.

I thought I'd lost him, but I followed the "clink, clink,

clink" I was hearing and found him across the room tapping on a tank that had a gauge on top and a hose leading away from it. An old oxygen tank, maybe. "Trident Aufmahide" was printed on it in a black letter gothic hand with magic marker.

"A voliar radioactive izotope mitts incleases der nutlitif value of der nitrogen bealing dipswitch."

I felt light-headed. The room was hot and close, the air musty and laden with something that reminded me of dead skin. The cats had the bird pinned in a corner, exhausted, beak buried behind a trembling wing.

"Der pelvic fin auf der vamale *Makaira niglicans* heated to von hundredt deglees centigrade. Und oil is ploduced. Vonderbar!" He hugged the tank affectionately.

Then he shuffled over to an old flip chart leaning precariously against a wall and began slapping it with his cane. "Der plocess is ass vollowz!" He flipped through the stages of lettuce development, beginning with an ordinary bunch of leaves. The second stage showed them burned up and caved in on themselves. The third showed a tiny, intensely green new plant rising from the ashes of the previous plant. Subsequent stops along the way depicted a race of giant, muscle-bound lettuces burgeoning out of the ground like a race of Titans.

"Let me get this straight. You spray that stuff on the plants and this is what happens?"

"Ezzentially. Ya."

"And then can they reproduce themselves just like that?" This was too much.

A cloud came over the professor's face. He shook his head. "Not yust yet. Zoon, maybe."

"Are they edible?" The solution to world hunger was before my eyes.

"Ach! Unvortunately dey are sometimes toxic to human

beinks. A vew haf unfortunately died as a lesult of eating dem."

"Then what's the point? I don't get it."

The professor looked offended.

"Dr. Beidermeyer, please forgive me. I'm asking stupid questions because I'm not a scientist."

He continued to look crestfallen but offered more explanation. "Der Plutonium additiff, und zimple booster, is der sticking point. I haf not come up mitt der correckt ratio." He whapped the flip chart with his cane vehemently. "Zoon! Zoon!"

"Do other people know your recipe or is this something you keep secret?"

At this, Beidermeyer smacked himself on his head with the end of his cane and switched to completely opaque, impassioned German. "Und" and "der" were all I caught, but the energy of his raving was awesome. One word, "Dirk," was repeated several times quite savagely. The tale he recounted was Wagnerian in scope and tragical proportions.

Finally, fairly depleted of wind, the old man sagged, head bowed, over his cane.

"So… what you're saying is that nobody else knows how to do this?" I thought he was angry because no one would pay any attention to him, that, as Dr. Greg Mendellsohn had said, the scientific community thought he was a nut-case.

"GADZOOKS!" the professor cried, clearly at the end of his rope. "Are you a halve wit, fraulein?"

"No, I don't think so."

"DIRK DOERKSEN! De scum-zucking pig! Faithless inglate! Since him, never again vould I haf gladuate assistants! Sharper dan a zerpent's tooth! May he lot in HELL!"

I gathered Dirk was one of those guys who never got around to finishing his dissertation.

But, more importantly, was Dirk the "Jerk?"

TWENTY-TWO

A woman`s willowy figure.

✣ ✣ ✣

I drove home fueled by the thrill of an impending chase. Weariness and lack of sleep were offset by the distinct impression that we were only days, maybe hours, away from a major break. It wouldn't be long before our tandem byline reappeared in the *Herald*, resuscitated, if not vindicated.

Off to the side was the irritating fact of Chester's abrupt disappearance. When I returned to the car, he was nowhere around. I combed the ag buildings and grounds only to later discover a note he'd left me in the dust on the side of the car. "Bye," it said. "C.D." Beneath it was printed in large block letters, "R-E-T-A-R-D." Somewhat after the fact, I realized that a passerby had added a leg to a "P."

I passed several hours on the Turnpike lost in a swamp of heartache over Ringo. His kidnapping had provoked a havoc of feelings in me. The very sight of another dog brought on a collapse of mood I was powerless to undo.

The account Chester had given of Bettina Bassett on our trip north also was aggravating. What was the amazing "deal he was talking about?" And not that Mrs. Bassett didn't have plenty to be depressed about, but how in the world had her mind been so suddenly salvaged? Since she had been caught red-handed with a large amount of marijuana, for the state to drop all charges meant that her cooperation would net them something bigger. Assuming Fendermann was one of them, who were the others? I still refused to believe Jim Walker was a serious criminal. Besides, Bettina liked him.

Something was staring us in the face that Trigg and I were missing. From the outset of my involvement in the story, I'd been plagued by the peeping tom. The more deeply involved I became, the more threatening his behavior grew.

Why me? Why not Trigg?

The more I went over the evidence and circumstances of the Devaigne case and its relentless doubling back to both Fendermann's financial plight and Julie Devaigne's wish to be rid of her husband, the more transparent everything seemed.

✠ ✠ ✠

Allison Highsmith and her Save the Manatee Dog Walk were going to be the end of me. The fulfillment of the divine plan for the universe, according to Allison, lay in securing the survival of the most lackadaisical species ever to tread water. True, I'd done very little to get the word out. But I hadn't been standing idly by reading my horoscope, either.

My salvaged answering machine unreeled minutes of pure Allison, chiding, rebuking, guilt-tripping. I punched in her number.

"Gaaarnit!"

"I know, Allison. We have, what, two more weeks?"

She shrieked as if knifed through the heart. "Ten daaays!"

"That's better than nothing."

"Where have you been?" Her voice rose to an especially annoying octave. "You're not taking this seriously."

"Allison, you couldn't be more wrong. But I have been working myself to death and haven't had the time to do anything else but occasionally brush my teeth and take a nap standing up."

"Don't try to tease me out of being mad at you."

"And don't play the spoiled little heiress with me, either."

"Nobody knows anything about the party. What's the matter? This isn't like you."

Unaccountably, tears sprang to my eyes. "Have you seen Chester?"

"Chester! I thought it was Ringo that was bothering you."

"I'm trying to get in touch with him about a story."

"I haven't seen him in days."

✠ ✠ ✠

Randy Trigg's hair, fingernails, eyelashes and eyebrows were gone. Vamoose. He was a mere nub of his former self. Sans these incidentals, there was something infantile about his appearance. Half-formed and barely developed.

"Nate Lynch has been around looking for you," he said immediately upon seeing me. Something Asian and sage-like in the way he sat on the bed, legs crossed and so perfectly hairless.

"Who?"

"The FDLE guy."

"What's he want, I wonder."

"And the sheriff is trying to track your butt down too."

"Did he say what he wanted?"

"Not just business, I would guess."

I spent the next ninety minutes filling Trigg in on the events of the last forty-eight hours. Minus the usual delineation of his features by eyebrows etcetera, his facial expressions were somewhat muted.

"So that old Beidermeyer's the source of this stuff."

"And his rogue graduate student has to be the same guy we saw in Homestead."

"The next question is," Trigg continued in a clinical monotone, "were Fendermann and the Mossbach/Julie team working together or separately?"

"Randy, you've gone cynical on me."

He twirled a pencil. "Julie's stopped returning my calls. When my questions wandered to marijuana cultivation, she blew from hot to cold."

"What I really don't get is how a man of Devaigne's street smarts didn't know that his cabin was being infused with radioactive gas."

"And it's still unclear how he died. Accident, murder, suicide. Pick one. An argument could be made for each."

Suicide? But Trigg was right. We were closing in on felons of one variety or another with plenty of motives. But that didn't prove anything.

But I was not the only bearer of information. The imbroglio involving the mayor of Miami had played itself out. "The goat died. The mayor was drunk. He's promised never to wear a dress again and has entered rehab. It's old news. Nobody cares anymore."

Trigg's editor was after him again about the Devaigne story, looking to fill the lull.

Trigg looked like an infant afflicted with a dirty diaper. "So this should make you happy. Why are you not happy?"

"Two words. Toby Lutz."

"Is he coming up here?"

"He's pushing him on me with coy questions like 'Couldn't you use the help? The guy's done his homework.'"

As I was about to tell him not to get so upset, we could work around it, the floor shuddered and the walls rocked. The picture of Randy's mother shot across the dresser and into empty space. A crack like a lightning bolt scoring a direct hit in the parking lot outside split the air. I found myself airborne and landing in the bed next to Randy.

I was on my feet and running before the walls stopped shaking. Thick gray smoke billowed up to the unit's door, pouring from a source just feet away. I took off at a right angle away from it, fleeing the insult it was to my lungs. Leaning on a metal support pole in the outside corridor, I caught my breath and a clearer view of what had happened. Flames rose through the frame of the convertible top to my car. A door had blown off and lay twisted on the blacktop. The windshield was gone.

A woman's figure was at the edge of the firey furnace, upright and staggering in circles. She was in the shreds of her underwear, bleeding. Without thinking, I reached to pull her away before the gas tank blew. I grabbed a thin arm and covered her as best as I could with the rest of my body, lifting her off her feet as we fled.

I ran to a small crowd of guests huddled next to the manager's office. Releasing her to the arms of a helpful man, I accepted a blanket from another. Only then was I able to focus on her identity. In the sulfurous light cast by the flames, Bettina Bassett's haggard face swayed like an eerie hologram.

A flood of uniformed men swept around us and we were separated. One moment Randy was standing by me as I lay on a stretcher, and the next Nate Lynch trotted alongside me as paramedics wheeled me to an ambulance. "It's going to be okay," he said. A damp sticky place was where my normally cool and dry forehead should have been. My left arm wouldn't move. Everything blurred and went black when the doors swung shut.

TWENTY-THREE

Swollen wet lips.

Music was coming out of a speaker next to my ear. A needle was taped to my wrist. Someone held up a mirror. My head was encased in a plaster helmet with a hole at the top, permitting an outcropping of hair faintly reminiscent of Woody Woodpecker. My left arm was in an ugly purple sling.

Through heavily medicated lids I slowly realized my hospital bed was surrounded by men.

Chester spoke first, and handed me what I thought was a tambourine, though the idea of dancing and singing at that moment seemed inappropriate. "Bettina Bassett wanted you to have this," he said, placing the thing on my chest. "I wish I could tell you more."

With my good hand I picked it up. Red hair clung to it. Was this, instead, some sort of tiara, passed onto me in a sisterly kind of a way, one Miss Florida to another Florida Miss?

I turned it over. No. It was Ringo's dog collar. An avalanche of anguished words stuck in my throat.

"She's had a bit of relapse from the explosion and everything. After she's rested, she may be able to tell us more." He paused at the door on his way out. "In fact, I know she will."

"Is he dead, Chester?"

His eyes bounced from the floor to the ceiling. "Looks like it." He needed a shave, but he'd changed his clothes.

"How'd you get home?" Tears ran down my cheeks, but I didn't care.

"I hitched."

Someone handed me a towel. I made an inhuman noise and a nurse on hall duty looked in. She picked up my chart from the back of the door. Lance and Nate, my remaining visitors, stood motionless, faces masked in choir boy smiles.

"I'm okay."

The nurse looked over my chart. She had brushy eyebrows, a puddle of fat below her waist, and steel-girded forearms. "Sure, sweetheart?" Her kindness and the glory of her forearms put me in a swoon of gratitude.

"I tried to warn you," Nate blurted, as if he were trying to absolve himself of responsibility.

"You were out of town or something, I was told." He had a cigarette behind his ear and had sat down in the only chair in the room, propping his boots on the edge of the bed. "We had a feeling something like this would happen next."

My eyes careened around the room and landed on Lance. His face was red and taut. His eyes were weirdly both concerned and vacant. "How do you feel?" he asked in an uncharacteristically high voice. "Can I get you anything?"

"Like what?"

"Oh, maybe a coke, or a coke and a hamburger. Fries? A piece of cherry pie? You know, whatever."

I pulled the damp towel over my face.

From a staunch cloud of Aramis, Nate whispered in my

ear, "Throw in with me. We'll nail 'em. Don't talk to this dirt bag." Then he pulled back. "I'll be around tomorrow, Miz Sullivan. Hope you're feeling better."

The powerful exhalation of lovesick lungs told me Lance and I were now alone.

"You almost died," he said, morosely.

"Tell me about it."

"Why do you do these things?"

"What things?"

His voice cracked. "The things that you do!"

"So what's happening with Bettina Bassett, Lance? I hear she's getting off, that she's started to cooperate."

"Who?"

"The old lady."

"You look kinda cute with your hair that way."

"Back to Bettina."

"Yeah," he said with a sigh, "That Miz Bassett, she's a tough old bird. Don't waste your time feeling sorry for her, Garnet."

"Tough?" He was raving. "Lance, that woman has had to live on the streets for twenty years. She has nothing to her name."

"Aw, Garnet. I know it's hard for you to accept, and all, but that old lady is a dealer." He'd drawn near the bed and was now stroking my topknot. His hand came to rest on my cheek.

The distinct impression of making intimate contact with an open-faced patty-melt sandwich next occluded my senses.

I sputtered. "I'm sick, Lance. Please, don't."

He pulled away and held the back of my neck with one hand. "Can I get you anything?"

"I can't," I recoiled at the sight of his swollen, wet lips, "talk now."

✠ ✠ ✠

The doctors, who came in on their postprandial rounds, said I had a mild concussion, a cracked spatula (or something like that) and a sprained shoulder. I was to take it easy for a week and drink plenty of water with my medication. Other than that, I was free to go the next morning, if I felt like it.

"What about the head gear?" I asked one, who had already asked me if it were too tight.

"You need to wear that until you're stabilized."

"Why?"

"You don't want to go bump that head of yours again."

"How long?"

"It depends."

Surely the *Herald* would pick up the medical costs and the expense of renting a car. Mine was totaled. I doubted I'd be able to replace it with what my insurance would pay. Vintage Volkswagen convertibles were hard to price. And too bad I hadn't availed myself of the group hospitalization policy ASPJA membership entitled me to.

These practical matters, though important, were drummed down by my anxiety over Ring and the larger, perhaps more metaphysical, question of what these injuries meant.

Randy picked me up the next afternoon, dressed in a baggy pajama-like outfit and a Chinese peasant straw hat.

"So, what's it, off to the rice paddies after you squire me home?"

"It's cooler this way, my skin heals faster." He thumped my cranial armor.

The question seemed redundant, but I asked anyway. "Something got you down, Randy?"

"Down?"

"Things could always get worse."

"They just have. Lutz is here."

"On his own?"

"Authorized. One hundred percent."

Randy hunched over the steering wheel as if the whole concept of direction wracked him with pain.

"We've got to do something, something big, Randy. You and I know what the story is. We've just got to somehow flush them out."

Randy moaned. The sound of my voice was not a comfort to him.

For some reason Dr. Beidermeyer's deep, umlaut-laden voice then sprang to mind.

"Randy, is Plutonium a controlled substance? You can't just pop in CVS or Walgreen's and pick some up, can you?"

"Forget it, Sullivan."

✠ ✠ ✠

Toby Lutz, the man, was something less than I had expected. The person who had terrorized Trigg with nightmares of professional humiliation was about as imposing and memorable as the average over-weight bank teller. Blond, balding, not as tall as I, waist flounced with enough extra inches to give the impression of being egg-shaped, he was a bit of a disappointment all around. Randy deserved an opponent worthier, or at least more intimidating, than this.

Worst of all, he was nice. He sweated the small stuff. He'd do anything we told him to.

He offered to help organize our notes, which on the surface was a considerate thing to do and would presumably quickly bring him up to speed. But Randy, in the grip of a profound paranoia, gave him a deranged glare as if he had offered to put a bullet through his head.

Randy called me outdoors to the parking area, which still bore the scorch marks of the blast, to confer.

"You've got to give him something legit to do, Trigg."

"I know it! I just can't think of anything I'd trust him with."

"Sic him on Doerksen and Mossbach. Maybe your editor needs a minimum of two staff reporters to be convinced about what's going on in Homestead."

"No! I'm saving that for us."

"You mean for you."

"I want him where I can watch him, okay? I want to be able to keep an eye on him."

"You better be careful or you'll wind up getting sacked." Then I had an idea.

"What about Fendermann's operation? Let him do deep background. See what he can turn up at the dealership. Have him talk to the employees and suppliers."

Toby was sitting on the end of the bed scribbling like mad in a notebook and didn't look up when we returned.

"What are you doing?" Randy demanded.

"Making some notes," Toby said pleasantly, standing up.

"About what?"

"Well," Toby gestured broadly, "you know, everything!" He offered Randy a glimpse, which was spurned.

Instead Trigg walked over to the window, stared out, and delivered Toby his marching orders without looking at him.

✠ ✠ ✠

Back home, I became wired and obsessed. Why hadn't we thought of it before? Far more serious a crime, because a larger (who knew how large?) hazard to public health than the sale of hyper-pot was the use of a radioactive substance in something intended for human consumption.

Plutonium 239 was the favored isotope of the fissionable radioactive metallic element Plutonium, according to an online encyclopedia, and was used in nuclear reactors and nuclear weapons. Didn't occur in nature by itself, had to be painstakingly extracted from uranium. And Pu 239 was a mega-potent alpha emitter that was easily absorbed in bone, making it a dangerous radiological hazard.

No one in his right mind would fool around with that stuff. Beidermeyer had to be all wet. No wonder all his colleagues thought he was nuts. Plutonium, my foot. *A zimple booster,* he had said. Fueled the inherent *(vonderbar!)* properties of female pelvic fin marlin oil. By what blind accidents and Nietzschean experiments did he discover this?

In an unaccustomed act of prudence, I called my old friend Kenny, the pharmacist.

"Is this a joke?" he asked, hesitating for the punch line. I assured him it was not.

"Yeah, and I'm fresh out, Garnet."

"How tough is it to get ahold of some?"

"Here? Impossible. Unless you steal it from the government."

"Why?"

"It's highly illegal without the proper permits and certification."

"Where else but the government can I get some?" Don't disappoint me, Kenny.

"You might be able to pick some up on the streets of Moscow or one of those old numbered nuclear research cities in the former USSR."

"Thanks."

"What are you doing Friday night? I've got some really good stuff. I'm talking interplanetary travel."

"Busy. Thanks again."Hold it, Garnet! What the hell do you want to do with it?"

"Sell it."

"Outta my league. All it's good for is making bombs."

"Or getting bombed."

"Have you been sniffing glue or something? There's no safe way to take that shit. And, hey, this isn't like you. You used to be a prude."

"Difficult times call for extreme measures."

"I just had a thought. Those teaching hospitals in Gainesville, they might have some. They do all kinds of wacky crap up there."

I searched all over until I found Julie Devaigne's unlisted phone number in an old purse. I knew I'd been saving it for something. I'd looked for it with a galloping pulse as if finding it were the one sure thing that was going to make this scenario work. But holding it in my palm, I thought better of calling her. No. *Call the nursery.*

True, I didn't have the merchandise on hand. But I now knew where I could pick some up. It was important to keep things moving, to have the ball in play at all times.

✠ ✠ ✠

Wearing a giant flouncy sun hat over my plaster-encased head and huge sun glasses, I called from a pay phone at the corner, just like they do on TV. You can't be too careful. Receiver in hand, I found the dial tone inviting, a vacuum waiting to be filled. When I finally stopped snickering and giggling, I pinched my nose and entered the number. My airways thus blocked, my voice had a sinister Eastern European, quasi-tubercular tone and texture, nowhere near my ordinarily feminine range of soft to shrill.

"I huv thum Plutonium pthfor you," this stoppered, sinusoidal voice said into an answering machine that had a cyborg sounding outgoing message. Then I left my phone number.

TWENTY-FOUR

Possibly useful as a plumbing aid.

✠ ✠ ✠

Under the cubes of florescent lights, my students' faces had a green cast. I held court at a desk near the bank of computer terminals that housed the "card" catalog and other electronic references, standing to provide a visible rallying point. With a russet scarf swathed around my white potted head, I cut an original, if not commanding, figure of intellectual inquiry.

The term paper unit called for one in-class library session. All surviving students had cleared a term paper topic and five-point outline with me and now were engaged in the initial rites and mysteries of "research."

We'd been hard at it for a couple of hours, I uniformly dispensing counsel and encouragement like breast milk, when a hush fell over the building and the lights flickered weirdly and then faded out. Only the red battery-powered exit signs at the four corners of the ground floor remained illuminated. Quickly they began to usurp my authority.

A murmuring rose among the students. One wise guy bellowed, "Now we're REALLY in the dark!"

A few students around me asked, "Should we leave, Miz Sullivan?" and "What do you want us to do, Miz Sullivan?"

I raised my voice to make myself heard. "Hold on a few minutes and let's see if they come back on."

"Miz Sullivan?" someone then shouted from a far corner of the room.

"Over here! Just relax!"

At which point a volley of automatic gunfire rang out. Roy Yate, of hand and TV remote notoriety, with whom I'd been consulting, crumpled against my side like a ton of falling bricks. My knees buckled and my feet flew out from under me.

"God Almighty!" he yelled. "I'm shot!"

I fell to the floor with Roy on top of me like an inept rapist. Then all hell broke loose. The murmur became a roar, pierced by screams of panic, the thud and crash of overturning furniture, and the awful whoosh of collapsing book-filled stacks.

The sound of feet drumming the worn carpet mixed with a chorale of moans and screams. A mist of fear-propelled spittle sprayed my face. One young woman became alarmingly rhythmic in her wailing.

Roy had quit crying for help when the class had turned into a mob. Dead, he was not, if muscle contractures and spasmodic jerking were signs of life. He was crushing the air out of my lungs.

"FOR GODSAKE GET OFF ME!" I screamed finally. And at that moment the power was restored and the lights came back on.

Books were scattered everywhere helter skelter, furniture was upended, an entire stack flopped on its side disgorging its contents like a tidal wave slamming the shore. Except for

Roy and me, the room had emptied of people.

"I think it's only superficial," Roy said to the ceiling. He lay on his back, knees bent, arms splayed.

"Where are you hurt?" I was on my hands and knees next to him.

He nodded toward his right shoulder. A small patch of pink oozed from his white shirt. "You all right?"

I tapped my head cast. "Yes, I think so."

White-faced, out-of-breath librarians then began arriving, followed by a nervous student here and there. I sat on the floor dazed. I'd just about had it with this routine.

The wall directly behind where I had been standing had borne the brunt of the gunfire. It was splintered with a crazy serpentine pattern of half-inch-holes. One of these times Dirk was bound to get it right.

Tamal Freeman's mocha face bobbed above me. "I saw him, Miss Sullivan! He knocked me down and ran right over me!"

Tamal had been returning to the library from a smoke break in the parking lot when he had been torpedoed by the gunman. Fortunately, he was not injured, and had picked up a shell the man had dropped in his flight.

"Average dude, coconut head, all hunched over. Looong, I'm talking long now, arms."

✠ ✠ ✠

Later the same night, after Lance and Nate had wrung me dry of impressions, I drove the anonymous beige Saturn I'd gotten from Budget back over to the beach to meet with Randy at the Palms. I felt a kind of progressive paralysis setting in regarding my sitting duck status as I sped over the causeway. Not that efforts weren't being made to catch the man who was out to get me. They just weren't doing any good. Moreover, Lance and Nate were engaged in a struggle to get the upper hand in the investigation, something that squandered time and energy. I'd left HQ in the middle of one of their spats. Lance had wanted to take me into protective custody while Nate wanted to place me under surveillance. Just before that they'd squared off over who got to keep the shell and run tests on it.

Randy couldn't get enough of it. "The stooges! See what I've been saying all along? What'd Dawtry say when Lynch told him he'd get a ruling giving him jurisdiction?"

"He said, 'Fine. You just do that,' then he held the door for him to leave. But I left first, so I don't know what happened after that."

"Don't know who got the shell?"

"Randy, come to think of it, I don't even know who's got the hand and remote combo that was sent to Tallahassee at this point."

"I forgot about that. But they're pretty sure it's Devaigne's anyway. You told them what was in Walker's paper?"

"I even made a copy of it for Lance."

"Sullivan, if we wait around for Moe and Curly to bust this thing open, we're idiots too."

"Who's waiting around?"

"What happened to your *chapeau?* The cloistered look really suited you."

"I'm much improved, thank you."

I lit a cigarette in Randy's pristine quarters and tossed the match on the bureau. "What's this?" A note neatly printed and signed "T. Lutz."

"What?"

I read aloud. "'I'm onto something. Possible major link to Mossbach. Have secured passage south undercover. Will be in contact.—T. Lutz'"

"Unbelievable."

"When did you get this?"

"Just now! I didn't know it was there."

"Maybe he *is* onto something. I doubt he knows he could get hurt, though."

"We briefed him."

"We didn't tell him about Trident Aufmahide."

"No need to at this point."

✠ ✠ ✠

The next morning, after sleeping like a baby now free of my ceremonial headdress, I worked the phones. A man in a navy Crown Victoria passed the morning reading the newspaper across from my place, but I wasn't clear on who he worked for.

I rang Chester, but he was in court. After some pleasant chit chat, I got Hazel to tell me Bettina Bassett was out of the hospital and back at Shimmering Oaks, where she had been when Jim Walker and another man had picked her up for an afternoon outing. That is, the afternoon before my car exploded.

"They got her in the crisis unit there," Hazel sighed. "She's all shook up. What she's been through. A dog shouldn't have to suffer like that."

I winced. I should hope not. "Hazel, is she really coming along well enough to be a good witness? Your unvarnished opinion. The truth, sister!"

"Yes, I think so. She can talk the talk."

"Okay, just between the two of us. What's she know?"

"You're not going to get me to spill the beans, Garnet, because I don't rightly know myself."

"You didn't type the deal?"

"Everything was handled by the state's attorney's office. I haven't even seen the plea."

✠ ✠ ✠

About four o'clock that afternoon Dr. Beidermeyer found the time to return my call. The hours we'd spent together in Gainesville had created a bond of some kind between us, I discovered, surprised at the warmth that came through the line. My heart went out to him as he asked after my health and work. He had to be lonely with no one to talk to but those cats. Like everyone else of any cultivation, though, he deplored the sneaky maneuvers of the press. But apparently in my case he was making an exception. After all, I was actually interested in what he did up there.

At the risk of puncturing this cozy bubble, I asked him to tell me more about Dirk Doerksen. I said I suspected he was involved in some heinous criminal activity.

"Heinous?" the professor echoed. "Vut else is new?"

According to Beidermeyer, Doerksen was the devil himself. On top of being a pirate of Trident Aufmahide, the professor had a couple of times walked in on him while he was torturing laboratory animals. When accosted by Beidermeyer, Doerksen only laughed and destroyed the suffering rabbits and mice by stomping on their heads.

"A disgusting mean stleak. Awful. I should haf turned him out immediately." He gave a voluminous sigh. "*Ach. Alas.* But I did not. He vas like und son to me. I vas und fool."

One day cruelty to animals will be taken seriously, if for no other reason than because experts now know it frequently precedes similar treatment of human beings.

I asked Beidermeyer to tell me anything about Dirk's personal details, likes, dislikes, background. I discovered his parents were Greek and had been in the sponge trade in Tarpon Springs and that he grew up around the water. He'd had a peculiar relationship with his mother αστέρι (er... *star*), Beidermeyer thought, a wild promiscuous red-head who ran off with an itinerant blade sharpener when Dirk was sixteen. He'd had no girlfriends whom the professor could remember, but possibly had a scatological fondness for sheep.

"I haf no ploof, mind you. Is only a suzpicion. Sometimes he vuld come in trowzers covered mitt wool. Und hair from other large animals."

"Dr. Beidermeyer, he's got to be stopped. You've got to help me."

"Is such behavior enough to put a man behind bars, Fraulein Sullivan?"

"Maybe not. But selling people radioactive cannabis certainly is."

"So dat is vut is goink on." Beidermeyer's voice hit a new nadir of despair.

I peppered him with questions about other uses for his potent formula and possible related products. Beidermeyer had already applied for patents for a Trident Aufmahide-based wart remover, hemorrhoid shrinker, mildew remover and nasal decongestant. He suspected it could be useful as a plumbing aid, but hadn't gotten around to filling out the papers.

"Und von other use, fraulein. Der calibration of der dosage is lisky, but at a certain strength, it vill vork as und love potion."

"Oh don't be silly."

"Ya, is good. Aphrodisiac. Vitalizing. Like starch. New rigor and vigor. Like Vikings they become."

"You've tested this yourself?"

"On rabbits, ya. A problem mitt fatigue and dehydration, perhaps. But unquestionably evvecstiff."

"Dr. Beidermeyer, I'm going to ask you for a very important favor and you've got to say yes."

"Anytink. I vill help you. Ya."

"Can I please borrow a cup or so of Plutonium from you for a few days?" I held my breath. Would a cup be enough? How was I going to avoid contaminating myself? "In a way, it's for an experiment."

"I see. Und vut elze?"

"I want you to come down here and talk to some people for me, back me up on some things."

Beidermeyer's reluctance was evident right away. "Mein katz," he said finally.

"Bring them along. All of you can stay at my place."

After a few clumsy phone calls, it was settled. Professor Beidermeyer would take the Greyhound bus and arrive in a few days.

"You might want to bring your swim trunks," I said before hanging up for the last time. "The beach had been beautiful lately."

I went to bed agitated. Was this Dirk predation a result of my own crazy red *hair*—something that had been staring me in the face all along? My own flaming red-headed image in the mirror?

If so, I could fix that problem in 30 minutes. If I wanted to.

TWENTY-FIVE

"We`ll have to sleep outside tonight."

✠ ✠ ✠

I ran into Lance in my parking lot the next a.m. as I was carrying a plastic garbage bag to the dumpster. A thunderstorm had swept through the night before and the tarmac was covered with warm brown puddles. The late morning sun was ferocious and the air was heavy and steamy. Lance stood next to his cruiser with the motor running and the door open. Something seemed off kilter, not right.

Part of it was the fact that he was dressed in his army reserve battle fatigues, not his customary forest green sheriff's uniform, and had a long-billed camouflage cap pulled low over his eyes. A wad of chewing tobacco puffed out his lower lip.

"Hi," I said, "Is everything all right?" My eyes fell to his feet. He was wearing knee-high rubber wading boots.

He motioned to the cruiser. "Get in, Garnet."

"I beg your pardon?" I was in a baggy tee-shirt, bra-less underneath, old soccer shorts and barefoot. Just before stepping outdoors I had smeared a triple-hydrating exfoliating beauty masque on my face. The parking lot was usually deserted at this hour. The masque had begun to harden and crack in places.

"Hurry!" He pointed to the cruiser. "We don't have much time." I started backing away. He had a nutty expression on his face. Something *most definitely* was not right. Then he lunged forward and grabbed me roughly by the arm. "I'm tellin' you, c'mon!"

"Wait a minute!" I struggled to shake him loose from me. "You can't just do this, Lance! What's the matter with you?"

Then he bent over and tackled me around the waist, shoving his head into my solar plexus. My feet left the ground as the air left my lungs. No more words would come. He threw me like a bag of potatoes into the backseat of the cruiser as I heaved to catch my breath.

Without another word he gunned the motor and we were flying down A1A. I clung to the wire cage like a frantic monkey and berated and pleaded with him, all to no avail. His eyes met mine in the rear-view mirror, then fastened the road. Repeatedly I asked him if I were under arrest, but he would not acknowledge having heard my questions.

He slowed some and drove within the speed limit once we were out in the country, and did not turn on his siren. When we came up on the high rise bridge over the inlet, he swung his head right and left, checking out the surroundings. As we swept down from the top, he picked up speed and then turned sharply right as if to go over the mainland. We crossed a low wooden bridge with a few fishermen at the railings, then turned down a gravel road that ran through an orange grove. Startled large wading birds and smaller white egrets eyed us from grassy drainage ditches as we flew by. The whirr of summery insects rose up from weedy embankments.

At last we came to a stop on the edge of a piney wooded area in the middle of knee-deep grass. Lance pivoted in the front seat and faced me for the first time since our sudden flight south began.

"You've gone and done it now, gal." He removed his hat and rubbed his eyes. "Detective Nate Lynch, FDLE, has a warrant out on you. Racketeering, RICO, trafficking in controlled substances. You name it." He shook his head.

Frowning, he hacked up a glob of tobacco juice and it landed in the sand. "Know a guy name a Toby Lutz?"

"Why?"

"Just that he turned your phone number over to Lynch as being the supplier to a sick drug scam down around Homestead. Plutonium and such." Lance threw his door open and came round back. "Don't play dumb with me, Miz Sullivan. I'm here to save your butt. Come on."

"I'm barefoot." Lance had me under my arms and was swinging me over his head like a rag doll. I landed jack-knifed over his shoulder and he started marching into the woods. With each lumbering step Lance took, I cursed Lutz and his researching skills. The guy was missing his true calling. He should be with the CIA.

My head was blood-engorged when we came to a halt in front of a dilapidated wooden shack. Unceremoniously Lance dumped me on the pine needle covered ground. He then picked up a long stick and went up to the door. With a flourish of the stick, he disappeared inside. A crow flew out a window and a rabbit fled from the front door.

"Damn!" Lance cursed amid a racket of wood and metal. Next thing, he too was racing from the building. He collapsed on his haunches next to me.

"Skunk," he said, slapping the dirt with his stick. "We'll have to sleep outside tonight."

Moving myself upwind, I took stock of the clearing.

"Forget it, little sister. This whole area is swarmin' with snakes."

Behind the shack was an airboat tied to a rickety dock on the margin of the swamp. Cattails, more saw grass. A dense surround of palmettos. I wasn't sure where we were, but suspected the swamp was fed by a brackish tributary of the Indian River. I walked over to the water's edge to get a better view of the boat. The greenish brown log that I meant to sit down on moved as I approached it and kept moving until it slipped into the watery grass.

The day passed with the slow imperceptible trudge of geologic time. Refusing to come within ten feet of Lance, he and I communicated with an amplification reserved for venues of public discussion.

In the heat of the afternoon, Lance leaned back against a pine tree trunk and nodded off into a sweat-soaked nap. The Coleman water cooler he'd brought along supported one of his elbows. I had been unsuccessful in prying his plan from him and had become exhausted.

At some point my senses were overwhelmed by a septic stench. Lance was over me holding a Playmate party pak cooler. "If that's beer or something, I'm not interested." I clawed at my calves and thighs with my fingernails. My legs were covered with red hot chigger bites.

"Better'n beer, Garnet. And harder to get," he said, offering me the cooler.

He flipped open the top and angled it toward me. "Look!" he said. "Surprise!"

Out of a bed of ice the blue fingers of a man's hand reached toward me, the wrist buried inside the cooler. Above it, in the lid, a TV remote had been secured with duct tape.

"See, he's after me too," he said softly. "I wouldn't turn this over. I wanted you to have it."

"I didn't so much want to have it, Lance, as to know to whom it belonged. . . And what it looked like." I pinched one of the stiff fingers and pulled the wrist out of the cooler. Yuk. Loose flaps of skin draped in scallops around it. The propeller took it off, as I thought. So what tore Devaigne's arm off at the shoulder?

"This is a fine how-do-you-do, Mr. Devaigne."

"I knew you'd like it." He touched my arm. "Chester should be here before dark."

✠ ✠ ✠

As the afternoon lapsed into twilight, a hot wind tossed the trees overhead. When we ran out of things to say, Lance's eyes fell to half-mast and he started giving me long sweaty sultry looks. Lance and Chester were golfing buddies. God only knew what that could inspire.

Lance was engaged in a pine cone-based flirtation with me as the sun squatted belligerently on the horizon, throwing long shadows through the spindly pine trees. It involved softly pelting me, at increasingly suggestive points, with pine cones, followed by animal growls and whines. Though the cones were sharp, I pretended to be mildly entertained and unaware of any intimate overture. When he began zeroing in on my breasts, I stood up.

"How about a fire? Wouldn't that keep the bugs and snakes away?"

Eager to please me on this one small point, he gathered up twigs and branches and placed them in a carefully designed pile. With all of the noise he was making, I didn't hear Chester until he was on top of us.

"You all right?" he asked, striding into our little circle of fun. He was wearing jeans and a tee shirt and carried his battered brief case. "How's Lance?" he asked, under his breath. Lance was on his knees next to his creation, trying to ignite dead leaves with a match.

"Chester!" Lance shouted, looking up, "Just in time for the beanie-weenies!" The fire then took hold and flared up, illuminating Lance's hollow-eyed, deranged face in the background.

"Be right back," Lance said, striking out in the direction of his car.

"What is going on, Chester? Are you part of this fiasco?"

"I'll tell you when you tell me what all this business is with Plutonium, for Godsake. Even the feds are getting involved, Garnet."

Just then Lance sprang back into the glow of firelight, arms full of canned goods. "Boy, this is living', aint' it?" He dumped the load next to the fire and hopped over to the cooler from which he withdrew three long necks.

"Not for me, thanks," I said.

Chester and Lance drank in silence for a time. "Ah," Lance said at last. "Nothing like a cold beer in the woods with a pretty woman."

Chester smiled ruefully in the firelight.

"Would somebody please tell me what is going on?"

Chester tossed the empty bottle into a clump of palmettos and began to rifle through his briefcase. Lance watched through slit-eyes, his face plastered with a peculiar grin.

"Okay," Chester said, pulling out a wad of paper and leaning toward the fire. "Listen up. Here's the deal."

Then he made a face. "Whew! What's that odor?"

"Am I going to jail?" I asked.

"Naw," Lance said, stifling a burp.

"They wouldn't take you with your face like that. No one would. But I might get busted on this."

189

"Listen!" Chester pointed to Lance. "You return the merchandise and Lynch drops all charges. It's the best I can do. He's got jurisdiction, Lance. You got nothing.'" He waited for this to sink in.

Lance then hit me with a pine cone just above my left breast. "It's up to herrrr," he said, burping and grinning. "What do you want to do, honey pie?"

Chester nudged me. "Your call," he said neutrally.

Strangely, I discovered myself to be ambivalent. I didn't crave possession of David Klondike Devaigne's rotting right hand. But if I acted as if I did, Lance would be put away and then leave me alone. "I'd like to sleep on it, guys."

Lance smiled and Chester's eyes opened wide in the firelight. "You *what?*"

"You heard the little lady, Chester. Knock it off. Give her some space."

Chester got up to get some more beers. His shoulders were hiked up around his ears.

"You're beautiful," Lance mouthed to me silently while Chester's back was turned.

"Okay. I need some background on this Plutonium thing. I don't have enough to go on," Chester said, handing Lance a beer.

An odd sleepy feeling flowed through my limbs. For the first time ever, I had Chester in a supplicant position. "Gee," I said in a rush of mixed feelings, "I'm not..."

"Just take your time, *suuuu---gaaaar--- pie*," Lance said, gutturally through an extenuated burp.

I steadied myself against a tree. "Actually, it was just a..."

But a whoosh sounded, interrupting me, followed by an intense tangerine light overhead. An orange day-glo flare had risen over our camp. Then another and another in rapid succession. Our little hideout was bathed in an eerie orange light that hissed, sputtered and cracked like run-amuck ball lightning. "The boat!" Lance shouted, grabbing me under the arms.

"Shit!" Chester said behind me.

A mad scramble in the dark followed and before I knew it, all three of us were in the tiny airboat and the huge fan was roaring like a jet engine behind us. My hair flew back, bugs smacked my face, and the tall pale saw grass parted before us.

More flares ran up overhead and shotgun blasts punctuated their swishing and humming on the upswing. I moved to the front of the boat and covered my head. *This is it.* The tortured sexy complexity of Chester Dare, up in smoke. Lance Dawtry's handsome earnestness, erased in the night. The fruit of mothers' lives, vanished from the face of the earth.

We ripped through acres of saw grass, maniacally pursued by blazing lights and gunfire.

Lance and Chester traded places at the helm so Lance could unholster his .38. He fired it into the churning back draft several times. An airboat came alongside us with a bullhorn. HALT! someone yelled at us from the dark. Lance replied with a burst of gunfire. The other airboat whistled miserably and dropped away from us.

Behind us searchlights swept the swamp. Lance took the tiller back, spun the boat around at a right angle, and we shot off in another direction.

Chester was in front of the boat next to me. He put his arm around my shoulder. Then he pulled my head out of his armpit. "What's that crap all over your face?"

"A masque!"

He turned to Lance.

The water began to grow deeper and clearer. The grass was fading away. I got up on my knees and looked over the bow, hair slicked back. The dank briny sulfurous odor of the river engulfed my airways. The narrow mouth of the tributary feeding into the river was just up ahead. A lighted flotilla was strung across it. I pulled Chester up next to me and pointed.

The boom of bullhorns and pops of launching flares began to sound ahead.

"MAKE HIM STOP!"

Chester signaled vainly for Lance to slow down. Then he pulled himself to the stern and they began wrestling for control of the boat. We were coming up on the flotilla of small craft fast. Boats of any kind don't stop on a dime. Even if Lance had cut the gas five minutes ago, our rickety old airboat was destined to plow head on into the flotilla at 50 mph. Its rudder was screwy and tended to stick in place, making it impossible to execute a turn with any precision, let alone shift into reverse, something that would surely flip us all into the water with possibly fatal whiplash injuries.

My adrenaline pumping at an all time high and my survival instincts screaming like sirens, I leaned against the port side of the bow, braced in sitting position. Our small boat rocked crazily as Lance and Chester lunged back and forth. The two had locked each other in bear hugs.

We were close enough to the other boats to hear the engines and people talking. Repeatedly we were told to halt. I crawled to the front of the boat and stood unsteadily in the bow, flinging my arms. "Out of the way! Quick! Move!"

The fight in the stern had picked up momentum and Lance now had Chester's neck pinned back over a big cleat, as if he meant to break it. I threw myself on Lance's neck.

"The ocean!" Lance choked. "The inlet! We can make it!"

Chester's eyes were bulging and his nose was running. I kicked at Lance's arm to dislodge his hold on Chester and threw myself off balance, landing on my back. From there I could hear marine engines gunning and shouts only yards away. I rolled over on my stomach on the iron-ribbed gunwale and wound my arms around my head.

Then, powered by sudden inspiration and the blind will to live, I found myself going over the port side, and splashing into warm black water. The move so surprised Lance, he let go of Chester, who quickly followed suit.

Bereft of his passengers, Lance turned sharply and slowed just in time to avoid wholesale slaughter up ahead. His engine coughed and died. Too hastily he tried to start it again, and succeeded only in flooding it.

Chester swam up and began to tread water next to me. He was struggling and weighed down by something.

"Here. Hold this." He passed me the Party Pak cooler. "I can't carry both," he coughed, holding up his drenched briefcase in his other hand.

"How do I plead?"

"Let me handle this." He waved affably as a boat pulled alongside.

TWENTY-SIX

Sodden merchandise.

✠ ✠ ✠

It was testimony to Chester's savoir fair, and extraordinary professional skills, that in a ten minute conversation with Nate Lynch in the aft section of a borrowed DEA boat, Lance and I recovered our freedom. The original deal for Lance still held water and Chester handed over the sodden merchandise with a flourish of fair-dealing and good-will. I suspected my liberty came at a dearer cost, but, as if he had read my mind or had known the truth all along, he convinced Nate that my telephone message on the Mossbach Nursery answering machine was only a trick to flesh out a story I was pursuing.

The one hitch was that I was now—as part of the deal—obligated to help Nate in his ongoing investigation, which had widened overnight to include the environs and occupants of Mossbach Nursery. This would not sit well with my colleague Randy Trigg, nor was it likely to please Sheriff Dawtry. But I didn't have much choice. In fact, I had no choice whatsoever unless . . . but no, once you're on the FBI's Most Wanted List, it's really hard to kiss and make up with them.

So I shook on it with Lynch. "Thanks," I said, genuinely. He squeezed a little too hard.

"I'm big on follow-through," he replied, as if I were not. "Don't let me down," squeezing even harder.

"Got a cigarette? Mine got wet."

Chester interrupted with an offer of a ride home, but Nate wasn't about to let me slip off without confirmation that he was going to get what he wanted.

"We'll be even when we've got some arrests in this, *comprende?*"

✠ ✠ ✠

Shimmering Oaks was a ramshackle affair constructed of natural cypress and set in among a stand of very old oak trees on a bluff overlooking the river. A private psychiatric facility, it had the look of a tiny resort, although the hush that pervaded the grounds bespoke tormented secrets and silences, rather than limbo, late night tattoos, Twitter newsflashes to jealous friends and rum punch. A loosely linked network of two and three-story buildings, it suggested a warren of whispery, stifled, and deeply troubled spirits.

Though I had entered at the right point, having parked in an area marked "Visitors," and had obtained Bettina Bassett's room number from a patient information desk, I immediately got lost. I passed a room in which a dull group therapy session was taking place, and everyone looked up as I walked by, disappointed I was not someone else. I ran up on a nurse with a drug cart outside a patient's room, loading a hypodermic with a concentration that made me swerve sharply and give her wide berth.

As I rounded a corner, I found myself sailing down a dim hallway with two white-clad orderlies marching toward me.

They put their arms out to their sides, and shushing and murmuring softly and reassuringly, said, "*It's okay. Easy does it now! It's okay, sweetie. It's okay!*"

Huh? It's okay?

I stopped and folded my arms. "I'm trying to locate Bettina Bassett's room," I said as sanely as I knew how.

The orderlies swapped looks. "Right, Miss Shirley," one of them said, "but your nurse is going to be very unhappy with you if you don't go back to your room first. It's time to take your meds." Together they moved in on me and took me by the arms.

Only minutes later I was forcibly bound into a gurney and wheeled into the presence of a nurse.

"Who's this?" she asked, quite rightly.

"Press!" I said. "There's been some mistake!" God, those guys were *strong*.

"Did you check the wristband, Harry?" the nurse asked severely.

"She took it off."

"This is not Shirley, guys." She turned to me. "Who are you?"

"Garnet Sullivan! I am a *journalist*! I work for the *Miami Herald* and other papers! I am here to see Bettina Bassett, one of your patients. Please untie me immediately!"

"Yeah, and I'm the Queen of England," Harry said, slapping his leg and laughing like the ignorant dumbbell that he was.

"She tried to run from us. She was looking for a place to hide," the other reported.

These folks needed to get out more. They couldn't recognize normality and sanity when it was right under their noses.

Still smarting from this insufferable incident, I was ushered into the presence of Mrs. Bassett by the obsequious and apologetic director of nursing.

I waved her away, "No problem. Happens all the time."

Mrs. Bassett didn't look too good. Most of her hair had been burned off and loose gauze smeared with a yellow ointment sat on top of her arms and legs. I guess she'd been given her meds because she didn't smile, flinch or even blink. I took a seat next to the bed and gazed around the room. Decorated in pastels, predominately yellow, I was remembering something about that color being the one most loved by schizophrenics when all of a sudden her warm hand shot out and covered mine.

"I never thanked you for the lipstick," she said clearly. She tried to lace her fingers through mine. "That was very nice of you."

Her hand had a soft, dry, papery texture. "Oh, that. Please. That wasn't anything to speak of." I swiveled my eyes in her direction. "Sooo… what's new?"

She hummed for a moment impatiently, and I began thinking, yeah, that's why she's in here, and then she said with more energy I dreamed she was capable of, "Don't think I don't know you saved my life, young lady!"

"Oh, I don't. I know you know that. It's very clear to me that you know that, I mean."

"I tried to save your puppy dog, you know." She turned her head to me. "Or do you?" Her brown eyes were something. So soft, big and deep.

"You did?" She sighed. "Such a lovely dog. He got away, you know."

"Really?"

"There's more to this than meets the eye. But you're a smart girl. I'm sure you're aware of that."

"Oh, sure."

"Everything isn't what it seems." Here we go again. Down the bunny trail.

"So you think Ringo still might be alive?"

"Very likely is. Out there somewhere."

She was a new Bettina Bassett, if volubility were any indication. But was she making sense? "I'm so sorry about this Mrs. Bassett. I just wish the cops could catch whoever did this to you."

"None of us is blameless, sweetheart. Remember that. You don't live as long as I do and not…"

The shadow of a nurse crossed her threshold. "Got to take your blood pressure, Bettina," she said, sweeping into the room with the squish of control-top panty hose.

"You come back another time, honey," Bettina said, holding my hand tight. "We'll talk."

✠ ✠ ✠

Toby Lutz was unrepentant. And Randy Trigg, perversely, took a passive role in my re-education of him. Though always eager to please his superiors, someone had gotten hold of Toby in journalism school and brainwashed him into thinking The Truth Shall Make You Free and that the T-word was ever allied with the PO-lice.

"We are not an arm of the law enforcement agencies, Toby. There is a critical difference between a journalist and an FBI agent," I said.

Toby sat on the edge of the bed in Trigg's efficiency and stared straight ahead with the blank demeanor of a prisoner of war. He still felt that I was implicated in the booming narcotics trade in Homestead. But he'd gotten in and out of the nursery compound undetected and had brought back notes on distributor arrangements that the Mossbach-Doerksen team had set up throughout the southeast. If his notes were accurate, the two were on their way to becoming the Wal-Mart of marijuana—with a catch. Over time repeat business was bound to fall off.

"Whatever you say, guys." He tapped his pen against his notebook. "So what's next?"

A hybrid noise, a groan-giggle, emanated from Randy's otherwise serious face. "Did you get to see the plants?"

"No, it was clear to me the atmosphere in those greenhouses was toxic. There were danger signs all over the place."

"That's too bad," Randy said. "They really make an impression on you, give you the full picture of what's happening down there."

I caught Randy's eye. "Toby, the situation has changed and we need to re-focus. It looks like we're going to need more deep background on Travis Fendermann."

Randy's mouth had fallen open. "What do you think, Randy?"

"The guy's a dirt bag sure," he said. "Question is, how big a dirt bag?" He slapped Toby on the back. "Go for it, little fella. Sic 'em."

That was all Lutz needed to hear.

"But don't go running to the police with anything!" I said. "Check it out with us first."

Toby nodded and was off, leaving me with an uncomfortable feeling. According to my agreement with Nate, I should turn over everything Toby'd gotten in Homestead.

"Happy now?"

"What's your problem, Trigg?"

"Miami wants something big. And soon."

✠ ✠ ✠

The tide was going out and the waves sucked at the shore as if the entire ocean were going down the drain. It was a sound in keeping with my general state of mind. I had been commandeered for the afternoon by Allison to help her spec out the Shark Pit. This involved a variety of mind-numbing tasks, such as roping off one thousand feet of sand, on the north-south axis, positioning and pounding fifty red fire plug-shaped stakes in the sand, and helping her decide where the stage and band would be.

For the last several days I'd heard radio PSA's. My own propaganda had already appeared in print in several places.

"What if the incoming tide washes your fake fire plugs out before the dogs get here?"

"They need to be deep enough to withstand that kind of flow, I figure," Allison said. "There's some big dogs coming."

Allison was keeping mum on exact numbers, but had boasted people were even coming from out of town, from as far away as Fort Mead and Micanopy. Those places didn't have beaches, but it was still a long drive with your dog.

Allison had given the program a lot of thought. She'd obtained Coconut Soup, a popular band from Lauderdale, for musical interludes. Their specialty was Caribbean and Reggae and their costume was, in the main, dreadlocks-inspired. For the doggy guests she'd dreamed up all sorts of contests and prizes, tugs of war, funniest trick, longest hair, most popular, best all around.

"Why does this sound like a high school yearbook?"

"I was also thinking of maybe 'best dressed,' but I was afraid that might encourage owners to dress up their dogs in hot costumes and I don't want that."

"What about places for the people to go?"

"Port-o-lets, they're coming Saturday morning. They charge by the day."

Banners, clam pits, sites for the beer kegs, lighting, electrical connections, the lists were endless.

"Muzzles, Allison. You should have some of those on hand.

And a water hose." She might also want to have an ambulance standing by.

"I hope you don't expect me to be part of the clean-up crew. I'm afraid I draw the line there," I said looking up the beach toward an undersized trash bin. A movement next to it caught my eye: two men outlined against the afternoon sun. They were waving.

"Chester!"Allison yelled.

Why hadn't I put on make-up this morning?

Chester and Lance had happened by on their way to our old campsite to retrieve some items they'd forgotten.

"Burgess is so excited about Saturday, Chester! He's getting a bath and his toenails trimmed. He'll look adorable."

"Lance says you've sold 900 tickets," Chester said to her, giving me a sidelong glance.

"They're still on sale and will be on sale here on Saturday too."

"That's more than $20,000, Allison," I said, amazed.

She gave me the tiniest look of annoyance. "Of course it is. Twenty-five bucks a pop."

"Chester and I were wondering if you two would like to maybe swing by the club for a drink on our way back. Maybe a little dinner."

I looked at Lance for the first time. Whose idea was it really?

"Deadline, sheriff. But thank you."

"Well, *I* can go!" Allison said with a cute little cheerleader bounce and kick.

Chester's features compressed.

Lance shouldered his way over to me, trying to cut me out of the group like a steer. "You're not still mad at me, are you?" He looked like a confused beagle.

"Lance, you're barking up the wrong tree." The words were out before I knew it.

He had a stunned look, as if I'd slapped him. "Lance, you're the first person I've told this to, and I don't want you to go telling it all over town. It's a very personal decision. But since it's come this far, you're entitled to know that I'm seriously thinking of entering a convent. In fact, I've already ordered my veil. It would be wrong of me to lead you on."

He stared at his feet and laughed. That Garnet, she had a million of 'em. "Ordered your *veil?*"

"I found a great nun website. Super selection, lowest prices."

It was better than an unspeakable incurable medical condition, but still didn't show much imagination.

Lance's eyes searched the receding wavelets of ebb-tide as his face bloomed like a rose.

TWENTY-SEVEN

Lead—or something.

✠ ✠ ✠

The Five Points bus station next to the Avenue B rotary at the foot of the causeway was something out of Dickens. The very navel of the underbelly of social transport.

Beidermeyer was late. I'd waited inside until I'd become dizzy from the bad air, and then retreated to my rental car. The clerk had been vague on the new ETA. The bus had broken down, or been in an accident, he wasn't sure which, near some hopeless little town by the name of Skeeter Lake, and the passengers had to change to another bus, which had to be brought down from Jacksonville. The image thus conjured of Beidermeyer, his two cats and Pu 239 afoot on a desolate Florida roadside was unnerving.

I made some calls from my cell to avoid a complete waste of time, but was able to connect with only my own voice mail.

"You still looking for a setter dog? One is stealing my trash every night. I'm going to have the pound pick him up, if you don't want him," appended by a phone number with a beach exchange, was one heartening bit of news. I called the number, but got the man's machine, so I left my numbers.

Allison called with her latest to-do lists and asked that I call her immediately because she was on the verge of a nervous breakdown with so much to do and "so damn few hours to do it in!" Allison cursing was a peculiar sound. She lacked the necessary depth of gorge to be good at it.

Roy Yate, my erstwhile student and the man who'd taken a bullet for me, called to thank me for the bromeliad I'd sent him. Said he was going to be late with his term paper. Knew I'd understand.

My landlord called to thank me for getting my rent in on time. Wanted to know if everything was all right. Then wise-cracked that I'd must have won the lottery or something.

"Miz Sullivan?" a familiar feminine voice queried next. "This is Bunny. I got a question about the term paper..." an annoying message on many counts. She was doing Jim Walker's work, where was Walker, was he in this as deeply as I feared? It was time to put my foot down. I called Bunny Knapp and told her voice mail in no uncertain terms that Jim and I had to have a conference if he hoped to pass EH101.

Randy had left me a brief strained message that his editor had "dropped the bomb." My landlord was too hasty. The single on-time payment was not necessarily a trend.

"Dumkopf!" someone then yelled in a racket of clattering bags and meowing cats on the other side of my car. The clerk from the bus station had overturned the cart carrying Dr. Beidermeyer's luggage and the cats and the professor were howling, seemingly in one voice. I got out of the car and began sorting out the tumble, first rescuing the cat cage. When I turned to retrieve the other things, the professor and the clerk were straining to lift a small metal box.

"What you got in there, man, lead or something?"

Beidermeyer turned to me. "Ach. Miz Sullivan," he said,

bowing gallantly. "I hope you war vell?" He extended his hand, ignoring the simpleton who was still struggling with the box.

I patted the old dear on the shoulder and pecked his cheek. "Welcome to Punta Bella, professor." Then I heaved to and the three of us managed to hoist the shoebox-sized container about a foot off the ground and lurch it into the trunk of the car, where it fell onto the floor with such force I was sure it was going to pass right on through and end up back on the pavement.

"My gosh!" Blood had to be coming out of my ears.

"She-YIT!" screeched the clerk who lost his balance and fell backward.

The professor looked down at him. "That vill be all, tank you!" he nodded and stepped into my car. No tip, nothing. He rapped the dash smartly with his cane twice and turned to me. "Shall vee go?"

✠ ✠ ✠

Dr. Beidermeyer's cats were named Verdi and Puccini and had all of the musical gusto and versatility of Pavorotti. They loved to sing and riposte with each other and the prof. They yodeled all the way home and the first thing Beidermeyer did at the townhouse was set the felines free. The tawny residue of Ringo was still about the place, and the cats found this an occasion for mirth, romping, flying and skidding across surfaces as if they were a couple of beered-up hicks on a holiday.

A Lladro piece my mother had given me of a girl holding a conch shell to her ear bit the dust, but I just smiled. It was a limited edition.

"Material things, heavens. What do they matter?"

"Ya, ya," Beidermeyer said. He was on his third beer and his luggage sat at the foot of the stairs. The leaden box remained in the sagging trunk of my car.

"Dr. Beidermeyer, should we bring in that box, do you suppose, before it gets dark?"

"It will keep, my dear, for a longk, longk time."

The allusion to its half-life gave me chills. "Do you think you'd like to take a little nap before supper? I'd sort of like to get you squared away upstairs at some point."

He looked at me with a tired, sad face and baggy eyes. "If you like," he said agreeably. One of the cats—Verdi? Puccini?—jumped into his lap and began to rumble and purr like an old jalopy.

Randy showed up around 5:00. I'd lugged Beidermeyer's stuff up the stairs after he'd fallen asleep on the couch. Pulled out the clean towels, a new bar of soap.

"So that's the big cheese," Trigg said. "The key to the secrets, eh?"

Trigg's capacity for unfounded hauteur was undiminished.

"You got my message, I presume."

"Chill, Randy. We'll figure this one out too." A plucky growth of taupe hair covered his head like a spray of finishing nails.

"YA, YA!" Beidermeyer then roared, trying to sit up. The cats stretched against his chest.

"Go get some cat food, Trigg."

✠ ✠ ✠

We dined on brats, sauerkraut and boiled parslied potatoes accompanied by several sturdy mugs of beer. For the cats, Randy had bought fresh albacore tuna. The professor was splendid on the subject of Trident Aufmahide and Randy and I sat spellbound during an hour-long lecture. If there had been any doubt in Randy's mind about the multitudinous uses, and the deadliness, of the mixture before Beidermeyer's discourse, they were gone now.

Beidermeyer was going to make a brilliant expert witness for me with Nate Lynch, if I could figure out how to bring him into the loop without ticking off Randy and ruining my professional reputation.

For dessert, the professor passed up the apple pie and asked instead for a single dollop of vanilla ice cream in his beer. Randy thought this an interesting German custom and requested his after dinner beer a la mode as well. The two of them retired to the living room with the cats and their desserts, and before I'd cleared the table, the professor had lit a foot-long cigar that was fast fumigating the whole downstairs. I wouldn't need a smoke now myself for hours.

✠ ✠ ✠

The hookers around Ugly Eddie's Truck Stop on the edge of town were the only signs of life in an otherwise deserted acre of asphalt covered with hulking eighteen-wheelers. In their cut-offs and tank tops, they flitted like butterflies from cab to cab.

"Maybe he's already inside," Trigg said yawning.

"He said between 1:00 and 1:30." We had been watching hookers since midnight.

"Is there a back way into here?"

"C'mon, Trigg. I'll never hear the end of it if I'm wrong."

Together we walked toward the fake log cabin restaurant. The counter was vacant. A wan waitress with fried black hair waved a coffee pot in the background.

"Shall we?" Randy held the door for me.

A blast of cold air hit me in the face and I walked into a tacky rack of Florida souvenirs.

"Over there," Randy whispered. "In the booth."

The tops of two heads protruded over the back of the ordinary truck stop booth. One wore the signature baseball cap with the carefully molded visor that had once graced my classroom. The other was shaped like a large grapefruit fringed with mouse hair.

"I'll wait here," Randy said, sliding into a booth in the back.

"No surprise there."

A stiff-legged march to the back of the restaurant brought me alongside the booth. It was impossible to think about what I was doing or I would have fled the building screaming. Rather than look into the faces of the duo, I focused on their entrees.

"Hello," I said to the scrambled eggs.

One of the men moved over in his seat and said, "Sit down, have something to eat."

"Oh no for pete's sake," a term my mother used, "I just ate practically a whole darn hog by myself. Go ahead though, boys. Pig out if you want to."

I sat down next to Jim Walker. "So how's it going? What's up?"

The skinny black-haired waitress appeared. "Coffee?"

For some reason I laughed out loud. "Of course! Bring it on! Coffees all around! It's on me, guys!"

The other guy snorted. I looked up. The poster boy for all that was wrong with the world.

"Hi," I said.

A fly landed on his upper lip and he didn't brush it away. Flat-eyed, he stared off across the room at some point over my shoulder.

Beside me, Jim Walker grunted, "About this term paper, Miz Sullivan. I need you to cut me some slack."

Doerksen was shredding his paper napkin into tiny bits of confetti. Light bounced off a big grease-slick on his chin. "Where's my dog?"

Doerksen stuck his little finger up his nose and extruded a hideous brown glob which he then put on the end of his fork. He lifted the fork and examined the specimen under the light.

With a light floating sensation I turned to Walker. "So how's business? Tried to kill any old ladies lately?"

Walker's adam's apple bobbed as he swallowed a mouthful of grits. He dropped his fork onto the plate with a loud clank.

Doerksen blew his nose on the bottom of his tee-shirt and began to smile lewdly. Bits of egg clung to his teeth and gums like spackle. "She's a liar if that's what she tole you!" Walker whimpered in mock frustration. "Old bat. Nasty old twat."

"My God, Jim. Your language. What's come over you?"

Doerksen rested his chin on one hand and toyed with his morsel-laden fork with the other.

"Get your elbows off the table, Mr. Doerksen," I said. "Didn't your mother teach you anything?"

At the mention of the word *mother,* Doerksen raised his eyes and glared at me.

Jim cleared his throat. "My buddy here was lookin after her whiles I was doing some bidness. Old lady's a magnet for trouble. Amazing she ain't been kilt in traffic."

Doerksen picked up his fork with the delicacy on it, licked his lips, and then in a flash pulled the top of the fork back like a catapult and flung the thing across the table. It landed in the middle of Walker's forehead in a viscous blob.

Fearing the worst, I dropped under the table. Feet shuffled, knees wagged in a flurry of rearrangements.

After a suitable period of silence, I pulled myself back into the light. Walker's jaw was set in an angry underbite, but his brow was clean.

"I thought," I said, "that you liked her. That you two were friends, Jim."

He shook his head. "She's had a long row to hoe."

"HOE?" Doerksen trembled with restrained laughter.

His neck crimped like an accordion. It was the voice from the greenhouses, the voice of the pit.

"I take it then that all three of you are acquaintances. Business associates as well?"

"I need an extension on that paper, Miz Sullivan."

"So you can continue your pointless self-defeating crime spree?"

"I need to get my certificate. I want a better life. I got Bunny and her kids to worry about."

"Then stop whatever it is you're doing and get to the library right now!"

"Bunny, she wants to be a vet," Jim continued, balling up his napkin. "Soon as I get out a college, I promised her she could go."

"The best I can do is give you an Incomplete. It'll become an F if a passing paper isn't turned in before the next term begins." This didn't make him too happy. "You must get with Chester Dare. He can straighten this out for you. Promise me you'll call him."

"I can't pay him."

"Pay him? *Nobody* pays him!"

TWENTY-EIGHT

Cats wrapped around his legs.

✠ ✠ ✠

Wary of another bomb attempt on my car, or the possibility albeit remote, of a meteor striking my car, and thus placing the state of Florida in orbit around the moon, Randy and I dragged the metal box of Plutonium into my living room. Randy pointed out that a meteor would have no trouble penetrating my roof, either, but I told him it depended on the size and velocity and I was too darn tired to argue about it. To leave it where it was and just go home.

Beidermeyer met me in his nightshirt at the top of the stairs, cats wrapped around his legs. The remains of my smoke detector were in his hands, electrical wires dangling to his knees. A cat batted an AA battery off the landing and down the stairs.

"Not a good idea to smoke in bed, Dr. Beidermeyer. What are you doing up at this hour anyway?"

"A man, a Mossbach, phoned vor you. He vants der 'stuff,' he zed. 'Und vut is der *stuff*?' I zed. 'She vill know,' he zed."

"Yeah and what else? Did he leave a number or anything?"

"Zo I say PU 239, is that vut you vant? Und he zay, 'Ya, is vepons glade?'"

"Weapons grade?"

"Ya. Zo I zay, Ya. Und he zed, 'Goodt. How much?' Zo I zay von tow-zund dollar buys und milliliter. Und he zed, 'Okay, you haf und deal. Saturday at der inlet. Come mitt a boat.' He findz you."

"Me? He finds me? Who does he think he called? Did he ask for me by name?"

" Nicht! Der lady mitt der stuff, is vut he zed. No name."

"Why would he care if it were weapons grade or not?"

"Is der best. Mozt potent. ZOOOOM!" He shot his thumb into the air like a rocket launching. "Bingo!"

"I guess this is good news."

"Von odder tink. He zed to come alone. Bling no von mitt you."

How, with the many and mottled boats that went in and out of the inlet on a weekend—the fisherman, trawlers, skin divers, drug smugglers—was Mossbach supposed to know me from the rest? Ohmygod. My hair, of course.

But where was I going to get a seaworthy boat that would hold the Plutonium? But did I need to bring the Plutonium? If this were a real sting, yes. And if Nate were involved, it would be. After all, I had nothing to gain from personally handing over a milliliter of Plutonium to Monty Mossbach.

And, too, me personally handing over the merchandise would put me at risk with Mossbach and his crew. But it would not do Jim Walker and Bettina Bassett, who were the other ingredients in this casserole of mad ratiocination, one bit of good.

✠ ✠ ✠

I was on the phone most of the morning with the insurance adjustor about my car. They were having a hard time coming up with its replacement value. I turned down flat an offer of $500 cash.

"You must be kidding! That car was a collectible!"

"Yes'm, it was of some sort, but unfortunately it was not a valuable one."

Then he made a snide remark about me having dynamited it myself in a fit of pique over a maintenance problem. When I pointed out how preposterous the idea was since the accident put me in the hospital, he said that was nothing. Some people had been known to kill themselves over repair bills. The matter remained unresolved. They agreed to pay $5.00 per diem on the rent-a-wreck for one more week, leaving me to pick up the balance of $5.75 a day.

When I threatened to change companies with my next vehicle, the fellow was cavalier. "You gotta do what you gotta do."

Dr. Beidermeyer, clad in a pair of Bermuda shorts, had left early and taken the kitties with him for a stroll and a look-see around the beachside community. I assured him that Weisbaden it was not, and he should reduce his expectations by about 50 percent.

"Perhaps I vill find some specimens for the laboratory," he said, and off they went in a sinuous shuffle. I did not expect him back for some time.

Randy Trigg barged through my door shortly after noon with Toby Lutz bobbing in his wake. They swept into the living room and collapsed, Trigg thrusting his Berkenstocks on top of the cask of Plutonium.

"Wait'll you hear this, Sullivan."

"I'm all ears."

Toby dumped the contents of his knapsack onto the carpet. Out tumbled notebooks and a ream of photocopies. He flipped through them and put them in neat piles, then looked to Randy.

"Go ahead. Shoot."

"Essentially what we have here is a guy in hock with virtually all of his assets tied up by another guy. The business, land, house, accounts receivable, the works, had liens against them with various timelines for repayment. But they were all cleverly tied one to the other in a network, so if the guy defaulted on one, he was legally in default on all of them." Toby paused to catch his breath.

"And which guys, Toby, are we talking about?" asked Randy.

"Mr. Fendermann and Mr. Devaigne, of course. Mr. Devaigne in the lender's position."

"And how did all of the loans become connected so that a single default could bring down the whole mess?"

"Progressively," Toby said, "over time, as Fendermann borrowed more and more money, and used the new money in part to pay interest on the old debt, Devaigne wrote codicils locking up the whole thing, tying it all together."

"And what is this serious looking wad of paper?" Randy asked, picking up a document with a large seal of the state of Florida at the top.

"A judgment. Against Fendermann."

"For what?" I asked.

"Pretty much everything he owned. The house on Riverside Drive, the dealerships, the land under the dealerships, his inventory, the dealership accounts receivable . . . I even think his lawn tractor is in there somewhere. All the collateral he'd put up for the loans."

"Because he defaulted on a loan and the whole house of cards came tumbling down!" Randy shouted. He jumped up and did a jig around the papers. He looked like a drunk leprechaun.

"When is it dated?" I asked.

"February 27th," Toby said.

"Two weeks before the maaa-rrr-lin tournament!" Randy sang operatically. "Two weeks before the sonofabitch died!"

"Cool it, Trigg. What else, Tob?"

"So April 1st Fendermann forms this new corporation, sets up his wife as the sole stockholder and capitalizes it with cash thrown off from his dealership."

"Cash that really, per the judgment, belonged to the Devaigne estate, am I right?" Randy had switched to boisterous side-straddle hops and military style running in-place.

"So what now?"

"Run with it!" Trigg said, saluting my plants.

Okay, it was a paper trail of a motive. But it didn't prove anything. Yet news was news.

✠ ✠ ✠

After Toby Lutz had been dispatched to ambush Travis Fendermann with the news of his impending humiliation in the papers, and so obtain some apt quotes, I forced Randy into a sitting position on the couch and made him count to ten.

"Do it again," I said, when the hoped-for result was not obtained.

"What's in it for me?"

"What if I told you I had Monty Mossbach lined up for a sting?"

"I wouldn't believe it."

"Then I won't tell you."

215

"OKAY!"

"The way I see it, Trigg, if in fact I decide to divulge this information to you, given its great value, I should receive something from you in kind. That is, I'm talking quid pro quo here."

"How do you expect me to promise you anything, Sullivan, if I don't have any idea what you're talking about?"

"Easy. Would you or would you not like to be present at the arrest of Monty Mossbach and his associates?"

"On what grounds?"

"Trafficking in radioactive materials. Possibly murder, depending on what I can scrape together between now and Saturday."

"Sullivan, you really need to get these moods of yours under control."

"If we can come to an agreement, I can deliver. It's that simple."

Randy stuck his pencil in his ear. "What are we paying you for?"

"The peanuts you guys toss me at the end of the month don't include hazard pay."

"So what do you want?"

"Not much. Just a guarantee that you won't try to cut me out of this thing when it blows open, that I continue to get equal billing, share the byline with you, on all of the stories." Let's be frank, I knew what he was made of. "And, one other thing."

"And what might that be?"

"A new car."

He shrugged. "I'll have to ask my editor."

"That's fine. Just get back with me on it."

"You're not going to tell me first?"

"No."

"What kind of car do you want?"

216

✠ ✠ ✠

I sat anxiously awaiting the prof's return, when the six o'clock news came on. I pumped up the volume when Travis Fendermann's shocked face flashed by, followed by a long shot of his GM-Cadillac dealership sign. How the locals got wind of what we were up to puzzled me, until footage of Toby Lutz's monk-like pate performing a vicious verbal assault on Fendermann rolled by. Toby frequently turned toward the camera and scampered fore and aft of his prey, trying to herd him into a frontal shot. The rascal was grandstanding. Afraid that his newsgathering would receive scant credit in the *Herald* when our story broke, Toby went public. If necessary, he could get a dupe tape from the station and show it to the editor himself.

A subsequent segment showed a local broadcasting babe trotting next to an angry-looking Lance Dawtry on his way out of HQ, trying to shove a mike under his chin.

"What does this do for your investigation, Sheriff?"

"Not one dang thing!" Lance jumped in his car and slammed the door.

Meaning what? He'd been cut out of it altogether by Nate? He had the low-down on Fendermann all along? The news about Fendermann was a red herring and someone else was about to be charged?

Soon after, a red-nosed, sandy Dr. Beidermeyer came through the door, preceded by some slow moving, sleepy looking cats. He carried pails full of damp, smelly live things and a hefty bag of shells, all of which he proposed to store in the sink and commode tank of my downstairs powder room until his return to his own laboratory facilities. Puccini and Verdi walked silently and stiffly with taut, distended stomachs, suggesting a daylong feast on fresh seafood. They immediately took to the couch and quickly became unconscious.

217

Beidermeyer, equally frazzled, took just a few bites of cold bratwurst and then begged to be excused for the evening, looking in on his carefully stowed specimens one last time before heading upstairs.

✠ ✠ ✠

The lights from oncoming cars swept by us, blinding us momentarily, and leaving us to wonder about our footing in the weeds in relationship to the road. Chester walked behind me, cursing the sandspurs and sand flies.

"It was somewhere along here," he said, as we came up to a beach access road, about two miles south of my place. "I thought he ducked into these sea grapes."

We stopped next to the shrubs and I called again. "Ringo! Hey, boy!" The surf just over the dunes pounded the pounded the shore like a cannon and a stiff wind blew salt spray over the dunes.

"Want to check the beach?" he said.

"Tide's coming in. There's nothing down there for him. He's probably looking for food. More likely he's up here somewhere."

An hour ago Chester had called to say that he saw Ringo dodging cars on A1A. He'd tried to catch him himself, but had lost sight of him on this stretch of road. It was in the general vicinity of the man who'd called me about a setter getting into his garbage.

We stumbled on in silence. These unaccustomed acts of consideration and thoughtfulness from Chester threw me off balance.

Cool pellets of rain began to strike us and the wind picked up. "What now?" Chester shouted.

I glanced around in the dark. We'd come so close. "That old house over there. Under the eave."

We took shelter on the front porch of a run-down vacation villa posted with "No Trespassing" signs, and sat on dead palm fronds. Chester leaned back against a wall. When the lightning popped, I could see his eyes were closed.

"Tired?"

"Thinking."

The rain was coming down with such force a mist was in the air.

"Are you ever going to tell me what is up with Bettina Bassett?" I dug in my pockets for cigarettes.

"I try to do something nice for you and look what I get. More questions."

"Just trying to make conversation, Chester."

He'd seen the evening news. He'd acted neither particularly interested nor concerned.

"Watch out for that spider," he said, lunging at a spot over my head with a stick. He beat the wall as if it were massed with nations of spiders.

"They were brown recluses. I saved your life."

"Thank you." I leaned into his side and he put his arm around me.

"I suppose there's no harm in telling my best girl the truth, provided it's off the record."

"Oh, this should be good. The truth according to Chester Dare."

"Are you wearing a wire?" He poked me all over.

"Stop it!" I turned my pockets inside out. "Do you have a match?"

"No and you should quit smoking anyway." He took my hand. "Garnet Sullivan," he began in his courtroom voice, "in her admirable wish to believe the best of everyone has overshot the mark with Mrs. Bettina Bassett. That is to say, she got old Bettina only about half right."

"Speed it up, Chester."

"How should I say this? Where to begin?"

"Chester!"

"I could start at the beginning, but it's a long story. I could disclose the most shocking items and let you fill in the tedious interstices with your own fertile imagination, but then you might err once more on the side of human goodness."

"Then keep it to yourself, for heaven sake."

"Okay. She was on the boat when Devaigne was killed and she saw everything."

"You're lying."

"No, I'm not. And I hate to disappoint you further, but she was a street dealer, had been for some time. Even did a little hooking on the side. Walker was her supplier and her john. That bomb business outside your friend's motel room was an attempt on her life, not yours, Netty. Walker and Doerksen suspected she was going to cut a deal with the state, which of course she was. And has."

"She was putting Ringo in your car when one of them tossed a hand grenade in behind her."

"But what was she doing on the boat that day?"

"Why don't you ask her yourself?"

I turned to him and tried to find his eyes in the dark. "So who killed Devaigne? How'd he die?"

"Let's head back."

TWENTY-NINE

"You'll never work for us again."

✠ ✠ ✠

Dr. Beidermeyer was wearing Verdi, his black and white feline companion, on his head like a turban. Nate, no doubt, found this odd. But with a lapful of Puccini himself, who was sharpening his claws noisily on his levis, he kept it to himself. We sat three abreast, I sandwiched between the two, in Nate's unmarked cruiser beneath Australian pines and surveyed once more the inlet's topography. We had just returned from a hike, in single file, up to the top of the high rise bridge over the water, during which both cats mimicked the great Gamboni's high wire act, using their waving tails for balance on the narrow railing.

Nate was a new convert to Trident Aufmahide. Beidermeyer's blitzkrieg of a presentation in his office a few hours before was awesome and Nate saw the light. When I followed it up with a briefing on how the chemo was being used innovatively in Homestead with cannabis and then told him about the rendezvous I had scheduled tomorrow with Mossbach, he fell silent.

"Press coverage will be key, you know, Nate." Two brown pelicans held their wings out to dry in the sun on a rock in front of us.

"Key?" he said, wincing at the thigh-pricking he was experiencing. "How's that?"

"First, it will complete the loop of his fiendishly complex investigation and bring to the fore the southern end of the statewide operation, dramatically showing the public the perils of drugs."

Nate nodded gravely and tried to pry Puccini from his legs. The cat purred loudly and held fast. "What else?"

"It will settle once and for all any questions of jurisdiction."

Nate made a sour face.

"And of course it won't hurt your career either."

Puccini hissed like the devil, arching his back, and Nate drew away in alarm. "My career? Why's that?"

"Why? WHY?" I turned to him. "YOU'LL BE A HERO, THAT'S WHY!"

Nate bit his lip and frowned. "Maybe we could get one of the reporters to wear the wig you bought."

I hadn't even thought of that. Somebody had to wear it; I just hadn't figured out yet who I could con into doing it. "Good idea. Yeah. Make one of the press wear the red wig. Use it as a bargaining chip. If they want in, that's what they gotta do." Trigg didn't have any hair of his own to speak of anyway.

Randy had already scotched any notions I had of going along on the trip. He wanted all the glory himself, undiluted, not to say, undistracted by my commentary. My excuse to Nate for being unavailable was that I had a previous commitment, which essentially was true.

"I'm hoping I don't have to bring in the bosses on this, ya know?" Nate said, confidingly.

"No! You don't want them involved. It'd spoil things." Trundling around a quantity of PU 239, even if it was encased in lead, on public roads, especially in recreational areas, might strike them as a bit daring.

"What if the suspects want to check out the stuff? You know, to make sure we aren't ripping them off? Nate was becoming the little brother I never had. A good egg, ready to do anything I said.

"Dr. B?" I tapped him awake. "What do we do if they want to verify the Plutonium?"

"Ya, ya!" The cat slid to his shoulders like a fur collar. "Zo let dem! But not near us, fraulein. At sea, on der open water."

"No! Wait!" Nate said, electrified. "That's too dangerous. Instead we let them take a hostage onto their boat. Tell 'em they can release the guy when they see it's good stuff."

"Weapons grade."

"Right. Then we bust'em. No sweat, see," Nate's voice rising with enthusiasm, "'cuz our guy is never really in danger . . . cuz we cuff 'em." Nate clearly had little brother potential. A weak mind, but energetic nonetheless.

"Yeah, and just to keep it simple, the guy in the red wig can be the hostage."

"Blilliant!" Beidermeyer observed.

⊹ ⊹ ⊹

The oaks that gave Shimmering Oaks its name, and which made the site one of the most desirable pieces of real estate in Punta Bella, massed together on the crest of a bluff overlooking the Indian River. There, garlanded with Spanish moss, and bedecked with cardinals, jays and mockingbirds, they provided a shady vantage point from which to view the barrier islands, the intercoastal and the causeway.

I'd accompanied Bettina Bassett there, strolling next to her battery-powered wheel chair, while the professor and the cats went off to inspect some lizards they found interesting. We paused beneath a clutch of trees on the verge of the bluff. The sun was behind us and afternoon shadows stretched across the lawn leaving the water before us bathed in yellow sunlight.

Bettina looked much better. She was wearing a pink robe and a straw hat and had made a rudimentary stab at make-up. Her lipstick was a little crooked, but her smile was brave, even and strong. Someone had outfitted her for a plate and her mouth now housed Hollywood-sized incisors.

"So when do you think they'll spring you?" I asked, after we both had recovered from the view.

"My attorney, Mr. Dare," she said in a soft voice, "thinks it'll be soon. It has something to do with the paperwork for the witness protection program."

"Really?"

Oh yes, it was all part of the "arrangement" Mr. Dare worked out with the state attorney's office. That Mr. Dare, what a wizard. If it weren't for him she didn't know where she'd be.

"And you, too, Garnet. I am forever grateful for all of the nice things you've done for me. Sometimes when I look at you I see myself when I was your age."

The hair on my neck stood up. "You do?"

"Yes," she said sadly. "And look at me now." Her eyes sought the water. "I hope I didn't offend you by the comparison."

"Don't be ridiculous. Heavens."

"I've had my share of disappointments in life, and . . . I suppose I wasn't as strong as I should have been. I let people

224

down, I let myself down. I threw in with with bad people." Tears pooled in her eyes.

"You don't have to talk about this, Mrs. Bassett."

"No, there are things I want you to know. I want to give something back. I know what your line of work is. Mr. Dare told me you'd be coming around again."

"He did?"

"Mr. Devaigne, did you know him?"

"No, I didn't." I searched her lined face. Light filtered through the oaks and dappled and splotched her cheeks. "Did you?"

"Rather well. Quite well." She laughed. "Too well, shall we say?"

This promised to be more than I'd bargained for. "So what kind of guy was he?"

"Nice." She sighed and her shoulders drooped inward like wings. "He was an okay kind of a fella on most days."

"Then why were so many people trying to kill him?"

"Oh, he had some problems. Can't argue that. What a maniac he could be. Bossy, mean. And," she giggled girlishly, "horny. You know what that means, horny?"

"Yes, I believe I do."

"No, he wasn't perfect. But who is?"

"Not me."

"Me either. He was a good businessman, though. Better than my nephew, which burned him up to no end." She looked out across the river and shook her head.

"What did you see on the boat, Bettina?"

She drew back in her wheel chair and grasped the arms with both hands. "Jim and I were partners, in a way. I guess Mr. Dare told you that." She glanced at me. "At least he told me he told you that . . . and a few other things."

"He told me just a little bit. He's real big on privileged information."

"Jimmy and I were trying to do some business. He owed me some money, or at least I thought he did. He had the picture the other way around. The matter was under discussion, shall we say?" She smiled weakly and put her hands together in her lap.

"Jimmy was doing some work on the boat for Mr. Devaigne. He'd rigged up this big winch for catching fish. Sharks, really. All electronic. Very fancy! Remote-controlled. I went with Jim to the boat to continue our discussion while he took care of a few things for Mr. Devaigne."

Slowly she unwound the tale of how she became a stowaway, fearing Jim was going with Devaigne to the tournament, leaving her high and dry and cash-strapped.

"You have to be persistent with Jimmy," she said. "You have to keep after him about things."

"Isn't that the truth."

"You aren't going to print any of this, are you?"

"I won't do anything deliberately to hurt you."

"That's good." She cleared her throat and leaned back in her chair.

After Jim had helped Devaigne cast off, and shouted good-bye from the pier, Bettina realized her mistake. She had hidden in a stowage closet on the main deck, just outside the cabin. Through the slats of the louvered door she had a pretty good view of what went on.

She caught herself midway into their reaching the gulf stream and back-tracked. "Well, you knew about the gas, I did tell you about that, didn't I?"

"No, what gas?"

"Part of what Jimmy did for Mr. Devaigne was set up this gas system for his cabin. He was really fond of that gas. It was something his wife had told him about. She got it for him. It was a greenish mist, bright, and very very expensive. Jimmy made it so it'd come out of the air conditioner vents.

Breathing it was supposed to make him..." she looked at me slyly, "well, you see, well... more of a man."

"You mean like hornier?"

Dr. Beidermeyer and the kitties suddenly beamed down at that moment before us. His shirt and pants pockets were stuffed full of squirming lizards. Bettina gave him her sparkly new smile. Some sort of transmission took place between the two of them. You could feel the surge of mutual attraction in the surrounding air. Verdi, of late Dr. B's head garb, hopped up into Bettina's lap. Beidermeyer pulled out a large chameleon from his shirt pocket and placed it on the back of his hand. In silence all three of us watched it change its hue from a dull brown to a ruddy greeny-pink flesh color. The tiny air sac under its chin turned crimson and puffed in and out like a pulse.

"Sit down, Dr. Beidermeyer. Join us if you like."

But he only smiled, walked away several feet and took a seat on a grassy copse under a tree just out of earshot. The cats took up posts as sentinels in the tree overhead.

"Where were we, Bettina?" Her eyes were locked on Beidermeyer.

Unable to rip her gaze away from her Teutonic dreamboat, she simply took up her chronicle in midstream. "Once we were out in blue water, Mr. Devaigne put some lines out with bait. He'd check on them, play with his remote, and then run back to the cabin every few minutes. He did this for a long time, perhaps a couple of hours..." A smile slowly brightened Bettina's face. Her prince had stretched out full length in the sun, his head pillowed by a tree root.

"So then what happened?"

"Yes, well, then a boat came up alongside us as he was trolling. Men shouted to him. They didn't speak English too well..."

"You mean they used bad grammar or...?"

"I don't know about the grammar. They were foreigners

227

and I could hardly understand them. Their voices were sing-song like. High-pitched. So then he stopped the boat and they came on board. I was scared then," she said, picking up speed, "I was sure they were going to find me. But they went into the cabin for a while. When they came back they were carrying tanks, like oxygen tanks. Then they got back in their boat and left."

I didn't know which line of questioning to pursue first. I looked up and noticed a small group of men moving toward us. As they emerged from the shadows of the oaks, I was startled to see Chester in the company of Nate Lynch and a tall guy in a grey suit with a grey crew cut.

"You are a popular lady, Bettina." Chester caught my eye and nodded.

"Come on, Dr. B," I called out. "We need to run along."

Bettina began to speak in a rush. "They were all in on it, honey. Every last one of them. Everyone wanted to be rid of him. But he beat them to it."

"He did?" Men were converging on us from all sides now. The law, the lawyer and Beidermeyer.

"He used himself for bait," she said, leaning toward me, whispering. "Sharks got him."

"Ouch."

"You betcha, honey."

"But why?"

She tapped her temple with her index finger. "He didn't mean to. He did it for *thrills*. It was just a game."

✠ ✠ ✠

I found Randy at the Palms hammering away at his keyboard and announced that I'd decided on a car. "A Jaguar XJ6, please. Put in an order with your editor tonight."

Silence.

"Randy? You listening?"

The clicking of keys resumed.

"I think I'd like a red one with barley interior. Sun roof, the works. Aren't they all 4-door? Whatever…"

"You're nuts."

"What I got for you is going to make you famous. I just hope you can handle it."

"Such as?"

"How about international trafficking in radioactive materials? Arms deals? Nuclear weaponry? That sort of thing." I tried to remain calm.

"No shit?"

"Plus the little matter of Devaigne's rub out. I've tidied that up too."

"Oh you have?" For Trigg this was tantamount to the garbage man finding a Picasso in a dumpster—and recognizing it.

"You come through with the car by tomorrow morning, Trigg. Then meet Nate Lynch at the inlet marina at 8:00 a.m. sharp. He'll tell you what to do."

"You're sure you're serious about this, Sullivan? You'll never work for us again if you're screwing around."

We now had an explanation for the nasty looking rope around Devaigne's waist. If what Bettina said was accurate, he was taking hits of hot cannabis and Trident Aufmahide for hours before dangling himself off the stern of the *O, Julie!* as shark bait.

The situation with the remote, though, posed interesting questions. Why did it fail to operate? Was Jim Walker, acting at the behest of the newly bankrupt Travis Fendermann, implicated? Were they aware of Devaigne's unusual fishing habits?

Another crazy twist in the circumstances was Devaigne's

229

trading in Trident Aufmahide. He must have known the stuff was radioactive. That it was loaded with Plutonium which could be recovered. And still he was taking tokes of it, ingesting it in at least two fashions.

But why was he selling it?

And who did he hand the canisters off to on the high seas? A sing-song unintelligible voice to the southern-bred Bettina Bassett could be what, Chinese? Iranian? New Jersian? Presumably he was paid for it on the spot. What then, happened to the cash?

The phone rang and it was Allison.

"One last thing, honey bun," she said, cheerily. "I need you to be a Puppy Cop."

"A what?"

"It's an honor, really. I'm only having four of them."

"If this is what I think it is, Allison, that's not a good ratio."

"You four will be a SWAT Team," she giggled, "the best of the best. Real Dog People."

The other chosen ones were a veterinarian new to the area, an employee of the animal control facility, and Lance Dawtry.

"Deputy Dawg, ya know?"

We four were to wear khaki shorts, short-sleeved white shirts and green canvas vests she would give us when we showed up. "And bring an old broom with you too. I've got first aid kits from the Red Cross for you to carry on your backs in these darling little satchels."

THIRTY

Pandemonium and Plutonium.

✠ ✠ ✠

It was red all right, but I was confused about the year. Late model it was not. It was a mystery to me how they got it up from Miami. Maybe they had it towed.

P-E-T-A-R-D. Certainly it had some pertinence here. But Devaigne was a better fit, if they were handing out lifetime achievement awards.

I rolled up the beach access road at the Shark Pit and the Jag shuddered, backfired and died. The ocean was glassy and the tide was out. A perfect blue dome curved over the scene. A few pelicans floated on the water half-asleep. Port-o-Lets stood like stanchions at either end of the roped-off area and fake red fire hydrants dotted the perimeter. The stage for the band had been erected in the center and two guys were fooling around with speakers and amps. Off to one side of the stage was a small white gazebo, Allison's command post for the affair.

It was a peaceful scene, rife with cataclysmic potential.

I pulled away from the shoreline and went to retrieve Beidermeyer. Together we would pick up Bettina and the two of them would stand by at my place, on call, as the deal and the dogfest went down. I was unsure if it was prudent to leave them alone unchaperoned, but had no other choice. They were set on sharing the afternoon's exciting tidings in each other's company.

If I never found Ringo again, this lonely palmetto-clotted stretch of highway along the ocean would always remind me of him. I never traveled this road anymore without straining my eyes for a red fleck in the bushes, an auburn blaze streaking across the blacktop.

✠ ✠ ✠

Lance, after learning we were to be comrades for the afternoon, called to offer me a lift. Framed in my doorway in his perfectly pressed shorts, face scrubbed and shaved to a handsome bronze, I couldn't help but think Lance was one heck of a good fellow who simply needed to be redeployed. He had a great smile. He knew the difference between right and wrong. He had good manners.

After bidding Beidermeyer and Bettina farewell, we drove to the scene in his cruiser. As we arrived, he turned on his siren and lights. "Puppy Cops! Hold it right there, lady!"

Allison flashed a dazzling smile. The sun glimmered from her glossy dark pageboy. She was a woman in her true element, ready for action.

Near the shoreline Chester was tethered by two straining leashes from which Pookie, Allison's Yorkie-Airedale mix, and Burgess, her father's sturdy black lab, lunged for the water and birds. Here and there members of the make-ready team were dashing around taking care of last minute preparations.

Allison handed us our vests and satchels. "I'm trusting you guys, ya know," she said with a wink. "This is no fooling around."

"Good Lord, Allison," I said. "We're a rather puny force."

"Where's your broom, Garnet?"

"I got mine!" Lance said.

"Okay!" Allison said. "You're going to go by quadrants. Lance, you take the northern quadrant, and Garnet, you've got the southern exposure."

"Southern Front," I corrected.

"Louis Flught, the new vet, is handling the area down by the water and Ned from animal control is covering the dunes."

"I guess I'm supposed to go unarmed, then?"

Steeling herself, Allison stooped and rifled through a duffle bag at her feet. After tossing out an assortment of frisbees and balls, she produced a beaten-up badminton racquet.

"Use this. Dogs don't play badminton."

Barks and whines behind us signaled the arrival of the first guests. "Now go easy. I don't want any complaints about unnecessary force."

Chester then walked up, arms extended like a wind-up toy. His panting charges bounced against Allison's shorts.

"They're thirsty," he said.

Allison's eyelids snapped back and disappeared like window shades. "Garnet!"

"Me?"

"Oh, damn!" She stomped her foot. "Now what?"

"What about the ice chests? Just take the lids off. Use them as water tanks."

"There's food in them! I was afraid something like this would happen!" She glared at me.

"Move the silly food. Or better yet, serve it to the dogs." I slapped the badminton racquet against my hip. At that

233

moment Coconut Soup bolted into a noisy, rolling, rendition of "Changes in Latitudes."

"Better get to work," I said.

Chester caught my arm. "When you have minute? Okay?"

"Why? What's up?"

"Not now, not here."

✠ ✠ ✠

I wandered through the hubub of people in tandem with their tail-wagging alter egos. Primed for trouble, I found, in the main, a boisterous, amiable group intent on having fun. Great Pyrenees paraded side by side with Miniature Pinchers, Dachshunds on tip-toe sniffed the rear-ends of Dalmatians, Pointers and Pomeranians sized each other up. Everybody peed in place, kicked sand out the back, and ears-up, tried to look smart, sexy, cute, and important.

A minor contretemps between four black standard poodles attached to a woman and a solo—minus his owner—Jack Russell terrier erupted in front of the bandstand as I passed by. The terrier wanted to whip the lot of the poodles, first to last, and hurled insults to the poodles' noble, mildly curious faces. The terrier was the size of a bread loaf.

"That dog ain't got good sense," a braided, guitar-wielding observer remarked from the stage, taking a puff from a custom-crafted cigarette.

"He drunk?" asked his associate.

"There's one in every crowd," I said, scooping up the calico brawler, who was gnashing his teeth as if his honor were at stake. I stuffed him in my knapsack, behind the first aid kit, and struck out again.

A sort of yapping hum settled over the gathering, a bass

backbeat to the Caribbean music. Sand flitted and hissed under active paws. Owners sipped beer while one of their arms extended unnaturally. Noses nudged yearningly for behinds. Lines formed at the Port-o-lets.

I passed many familiar faces, all of which wore the benign expression of being in the company of one's best friend. Everyone had on a sticker of a manatee and her calf, evidence of having paid twenty-five dollars for the pleasure of the afternoon. This was a brilliant idea on Allison's part, after all.

Rounding the southern terminus of my assigned territory, I ran into Bunny Knapp with two tow-haired toddlers and a prime specimen of an American Brown Dog. As a veterinarian wannabe, her heart was in the right place, but her financing was suspect. Bunny raised her voice over the yapper in my backpack. "He's gonna have his term paper in on time, Miz Sullivan!"

The games and contests had begun on the packed sand near the water and Allison's voice piped over the loudspeakers, marshalling contestants and awarding ribbons. Frisbees were flung, dogs soared into the air and nipped them from impossible altitudes. Races were run and tricks performed to a raucous backdrop of laughter, barking and applause.

Allison was assisted throughout by an attentive Lance Dawtry, who was the recipient, in turn, of several of her special smiles.

Finally, as the sun dropped to the top of the dunes behind us, the aroma of fresh seafood wafted over the crowd. The yip and haw of human raconteuring grew louder but a whiney tense hush settled over the dogs. I looked around. Stalactites of drool everywhere. After a squirm and a thrust at my shoulder blades, I was five pounds lighter.

Guided by their dogs, guests gravitated to the buffets while the band played a reggae version of dinner music. I meandered around the abandoned party grounds, picking up stray cups and retrieving a brown pile here and there with my racquet.

Thus busied, I ran up on Chester, foot poised on the steps of the gazebo, picking with a stick at a dark mass impaled on his toes. Pookie and Burgess were stretched out in the shadow of the gazebo, legs extended as if dead.

I felt my pocket for my phone. Beidermeyer was on strict instructions to call if anything developed with the sting, something that surely was taking place by this point. Sundown was only an hour or so away.

"Sit down for a minute," Chester said without looking up.

"Whatever it is, I didn't do it."

"I hope you know I know what's going on," he said, scraping a glob of amber from his big toe.

"How's that?"

"Whatever Bettina told you the other day, don't print it," Chester said. "That was for your benefit only, understand? The net is only recently cast, get me?"

"Why is she in a witness protection program, Chester?" Everything had a price.

"She needs protection. And she's a valuable witness." He rolled onto the sand beside me and furiously rubbed his foot with a discarded candy wrapper.

"It's international arm deals, trafficking in radioactive materials, that sort of thing, isn't it?"

He looked at me. "No."

"But she saw Devaigne pass Trident Aufmahide to foreign agents when she was on his boat!"

"Garnet, tell me this," he asked with belabored patience. "Why would David Devaigne want to get himself mixed up in something like that? He was already stinking rich."

"Yes, but he was crazy too."

"Not that crazy." Someone disciplined a pooch across

the way and the yelping of hurt feelings split the air. "Those were fishing buddies of his that came aboard, out in the tournament themselves. One of them a CEO of a Brooklyn-based consumer products company. He wanted to give him samples of the stuff for possible commercial development. You know, package it as a vitalizing inhaler or tonic. He left a paper trail about it in his personal correspondence."

I felt a pinprick open in my story plans. "What about the money she found?"

"What money? Devaigne took in exchange a bottle of hundred year-old cognac."

"Then he didn't know it was radioactive." I was deflating rapidly.

"Garnet, the issues here are drugs, stolen cars and illegal use of hazardous materials, the whole ball of wax with probable connections to organized crime."

"Organized crime?" This wasn't so bad after all. A thought occurred to me: call Julie Devaigne, "Let's do lunch," drive down in my Jag, get her side of the story—girl-to-girl.

"Another thing," Chester said, interrupting my backing and filling. "I know you've noticed a change, shall we say, in my comportment. I want you to know I'm seeing someone."

I fell back against the two dog carcasses. "Oh?"

"Yeah. He's helped me, I think. What do you think?"

I released Pookie and Burgess and threw myself at Chester. "This makes me so happy."

"You wouldn't give up."

"I tried."

"I'm sorry."

"Don't be."

"Things are going to be different."

"They are already."

A vibration on my hip got my attention.

"Dey are coming, fraulein! Vatch der oshen!" Beidermeyer

exclaimed. He sounded as if he were doing backflips.

My eyes searched the fading blue horizon. Two or three glinting specks were coming up out of the south, engines muffled by the distance. "I think I see," I said.

"Und *vee* are coming too!" Beidermeyer declared in a spasm of joy.

The spectacle of Dr. B, legs encased in cat buskins, with Bettina Bassett on his arm was unambiguously alarming under the circumstances. "No, don't do that!"

"Vee haf und announzement to make, ya!" he said, hanging up with a bang. I rocked back in the sand, one arm looped through Chester's. *Bettina Beidermeyer*, it had a nice, sonorous, feminine swish to it.

"My God we're in for it now!" I said, springing to my feet.

The boats surged into view offshore. A chrome-sided narrow Cigarette was in the lead, at the prow of which sat a lustrous red-head, shoulder-length hair standing out straight behind him in the gale. Arms resolutely at his sides, head leaning ferociously into the wind, Trigg cut a striking figure of journalistic bravado.

Two larger sluggish crafts with whirling blue bubbles on top brought up the rear. Amidst a burst of gunfire I spotted a figure in a billowing trench coat in the stern of one boat, arms waving madly. Behind him rocked Toby Lutz, eye stuck to his camera like a suction cup.

Chester stood by my side, preternaturally silent, but supportive.

From the south another craft buzzed into view, a small flat-bottomed bass boat. Its captain wore a blue shirt and ball cap. He cut his engine near the shore to watch the others roar by. As they did, he lifted his cap and scratched his head. Then he revved up his outboard and took off in the opposite direction, flinging a scornful rooster tail of water at anyone who cared to notice.

A long tubular structure—a rocket launcher?—was subsequently hurried into the aft section of the now crazily circling Cigarette. The artillery was jerked around the pitching deck by a man with very long arms and a bowling ball for a head. Leveled at its pursuers, it recoiled spastically off target. Fire spilled harmlessly through the twilit sky.

Dully, I became aware of a deep oceanic crescendo of canine voices. I felt around for my racquet. A wild hue and cry went up, telescoping toward the dunes above us. Beidermeyer and his bride had arrived, adorned with Verdi and Puccini. I clenched my weapon and prayed they could be light on their feet and that they'd asked the taxi to wait.

As the stars came out overhead, a pandemonium of pet owners gave chase, shouting an unintelligible host of dog names. Like a violent storm, the terrible racket assaulted the heavens and drifted, gradually, into the distance.

At some imponderable point, with my eyes frozen shut against the press of events, a drippy ice cube rudely prodded the back of my knee. I spun around, loosing myself from Chester, and took ninety pounds of a big red wet hairy thing into my arms. As I sank to my knees in the sand covered in wet kisses, the hot tears began to flow. My Ringo was back. Dirty, smelly and skinny, but back. I fell into a sandy swoon of bliss. With my warm man in one arm and my warm dog in the other, it would be days—maybe weeks—before I would find something else to ring my bell and pursue as if my life depended on it—let alone get arrested for. I hoped I wouldn't die of boredom and undiluted happiness in the interval.∎

Stay Tuned!

Find series updates, Garnet Live from Florida trivia,
Florida lore, and free, short humorous pieces
by
Margaret Jean Langstaff
on Garnet's blog www.garnetsullivanlivefromflorida.com.
Look for the second novel of Garnet's escapades and
misadventures early in 2011.

Diva continues Garnet's madcap search for headlines and news during Florida's sinister hurricane season. Think harrowing weather, stormy women, and wild romantic trysts as Garnet breaks into broadcast journalism!

www.ingramcontent.com/pod-product-compliance
Lightning Source LLC
Chambersburg PA
CBHW070917180626
46817CB00003B/1095